# One of a Kind Love

## Athena Dent

PublishAmerica
Baltimore

PublishAmerica has allowed this work to remain exactly as the author intended, verbatim, without editorial input.

Hardcover 978-1-4512-3034-5
Softcover 978-1-4512-3035-2
PUBLISHED BY PUBLISHAMERICA, LLLP
www.publishamerica.com
Baltimore

Printed in the United States of America

For those

who want

to **LOVE**

Honestly,

Peacefully,

Respectfully,

Sincerely,

through the **SPIRIT**

**LOVE** IS…

A HIT
OR A MISS

A SIGH
OR A SCREAM

A SMILE
OR A FROWN

A HUG
OR SPACE

GIVE
OR TAKE

**LOVE** IS…
        EXACTLY

# One

For some people; love is not just an emotion, but a principle. To dedicate one's self to another human being, to trust what is unseen of the union of two spirits and lastly to hold on for what may be an **unforgettable** ride. Some of us forget to wear out seatbelts, but for Crystal and Carlos; it turns out to be quite a ride, a **VERY ROUGH** ride.

\*\*\*

It has always been a calling for Crystal to become a Police officer and to add a little spice to her job—an Undercover. Today was just like any other day, but it would be a day that would *change* many days to come.

It's a beautiful Monday morning as Crystal enters the large conference room at the precinct to attend roll call. Every police officer who works the morning shift is in attendance, including Carlos. Carlos is a handsome, smart officer who has a sense of humor to go along with his 'well put together' package. Crystal has been friends with Carlos for the past six years and there are times she wishes they were *more* than that.

"Good morning, everyone", the Sergeant clears his throat. "We are going to start off this morning with a new rotation. The person that you will be paired off with today will be your partner for one year". The Sergeant fixes his glasses before reading from a sheet of paper that has the names of the officers at the precinct. The conference room is crowded as usual and everyone is hyped about who will be with whom.

Crystal already knows who she wants to be with and as she looks around the room, she sees Carlos looking at her and he winks at her. She smiles back and in turn, he gives her a gracious smile.

The Sergeant continues, "Okay everyone, please listen for your names and once I'm finished, you can meet up with your partners outside in the lobby. I can tell all of you are SO excited". The Sergeant has a grin on his face. Everybody in the room laughs. "Debra and Chris, Maria and Jonathan, Rose and Malcolm, Crystal and…Carlos and since there are two Carlos's here, let me be specific. Carlos Ruiz". Both Crystal and Carlos have the **BIGGEST** koolaid smiles on their faces as they look at one another.

"Okay everyone, be nice to each other and keep your eyes on your partner. Oh yeah, let's be careful out there. Dismissed". Everyone starts leaving the conference room slowly.

Some of the officers are pleased with their new partners, while the *LOOK* of others tell otherwise. Crystal and Carlos meet up in the hallway. They exchange handshakes.

"Hi, Crystal. How's it going?", Carlos says while still smiling. "I'm fine", Crystal is still grinning from ear to ear. Carlos is saying in the back of his mind—**BOY OH BOY, I AM THE LUCKIEST MAN IN THE WORLD!**. Carlos moves closer to Crystal,"I guess we got lucky, uh?".

"I guess so", Crystal still has that koolaid smile on her face.

"The good thing is that we already know each other pretty well. Can you imagine two rookies starting off fresh?", Crystal fixes her belt.

"Yeah, I know. Well, are you ready to hit the road?", Carlos puts his hand out. "Ready when you are, partner",

Crystal slaps him a 'high five'. They leave the precinct and walk towards one of the police cars.

"It's a beautiful day. The weather forecaster said that it should be a sunny day, all day", Crystal blocks the sun from her eyes by putting on her glasses. "Good. It will give me a chance to work on my tan", Carlos smiles at Crystal.

"How are you going to get a tan, through your clothes?", Crystal says jokingly.

"We do get lunch breaks", Carlos says this sarcastically. "Do you plan on going to the beach?", Crystal raises her eyebrows.

"You never know", Carlos starts chuckling. "Yeah, right", Crystal laughs back. They stop in front of one of the unmarked cars. Carlos gets in the driver's seat and Crystal sits in the passenger seat. Crystal turns on the police radio. As they put on their seatbelts, an announcement comes over the radio-

'There is a robbery in progress at Wall street, near Federal Hall. There are four suspects in a bank and they are armed'.

Carlos turns on the ignition, "Well, the party seems to be getting started". He backs out of the parking space, steps on the gas and takes off. Crystal looks at him wondering how their first day will turn out. With sirens **BLARING,** they eventually arrive to Federal Hall. They get out of their unmarked car and walk over to where three other marked police cars are stationed outside the bank. There is a crowd gathered around the bank, but they are being kept back by police barricades.

"Boy, people love excitement", Carlos looks over at Crystal. "Too much excitement, if you ask me", Crystal shakes her head. Carlos and Crystal walk over to two of the officers,

"What's going on inside the bank?", Carlos says with a concerned look on his face as he shakes one of the officer's hand.

"There are four suspects inside the bank and about 20 customers", the officer quickly responds. "They are not customers anymore, they are hostages", Crystal says to the officer.

Crystal looks over at the bank, "Has anyone spoken to any of the gunmen?". The other officer responds, "No, not yet. We just arrived here five minutes ago". Crystal looks concerned, because she knows time is precious in a situation like this. "Well, let's get one of them talking. Do you have a bullhorn?", Crystal asks the officer. "Yes we do", one of the officers tells her before going to his car. He opens the trunk and takes out a bullhorn.

He walks back over to where Carlos and Crystal are. Carlos pauses for a minute before he responds to the officer, "Let them know that we are willing to negotiate for the release of the hostages. We don't want any of them getting trigger happy. Let's try to keep their heads cool".

The officer gets on the bullhorn, "To the suspects inside…we are willing to negotiate for the release of the hostages. We do not want anyone harmed. We would like to send someone in, so that you can give your demands. If you understand, please send one of your men to the front door".

Carlos looks at the officer, "That was good. Let's just hope we are dealing with rational people". "How rational can you be, if you are holding hostages", Crystal looks at Carlos with her eyebrows raised. Carlos nods his head, "You're right".

Everybody looks at one another; then all of a sudden, the door to the bank opens and a man with a ninja-style mask on peaks out the door holding a hostage.

The hostage is a little girl about six years old. In his other hand, he holds a machine gun. Carlos squints his eyes, "The gunman looks like a kid himself". One of the officers responds, "Well he may be a kid, but he knows exactly what he is doing". "Maybe not. He could be just going along for the ride", Carlos shakes his head. Crystal has a *puzzled* look on her face. As she looks closely at the gunman, she realizes it is someone she knows, "Raymond?".

Carlos turns to Crystal, "Something wrong?". Crystal responds slowly, "Yeah". The gunman speaks, "We've got 20 hostages in here. We will let five go for now, That's it!. We will let the rest go, when we get our demands met. You can send in two cops, unarmed. Don't try anything stupid!". The little girl is crying and holding a doll. The suspect goes back inside the bank and closes the door.

Crystal turns to Carlos, "I know that kid". Carlos looks at Crystal as if she is joking, "You're kidding, right?".

"No, I'm not kidding. I recognize that voice. I know him very well. His name is Raymond Start. He grew up in my old neighborhood. I remember when he was a little baby".

"This should be easy", Carlos says sarcastically. "Don't be so sure", Crystal looks at Carlos with much concern on her face. Carlos turns to the other two officers, "I think we should wait, until the Sergeant gets here".

No sooner than he said that, the Sergeant pulls up in his car. He exits his car and walks over to where Crystal, Carlos and the other two officers are standing. "Alright folks, what's the good news?", the Sergeant pats Crystal on the back.

Carlos responds, "Well, let me give you the BAD news first. We've got four suspects and 20 hostages. The good news is that Crystal knows one of the suspects".

The Sergeant looks at Crystal with his eyebrows raised, "Really". Crystal takes a deep breath, "Unfortunately, I do. He's a kid from my old neighborhood. His name is Raymond Start".

One of the officers responds, "How were you able to recognize him with that mask on?". Crystal turns to the officer, "His eyes and then when he started talking, I knew it was him".

The Sergeant turns to one of the officers, "See if you can get any additional information on Mr. Start". "You got it, Sarge", the officer immediately leaves. The Sergeant looks back at Crystal, "Well, this could be a good thing. Maybe it will make things go a little easier".

"The suspect said that they would release five hostages after we send in two unarmed officers", Crystal says this with a bit of enthusiasm. Crystal adds quickly, "Oh one more thing, Sarge. There are children inside. At least one we know of for sure". "Great", the Sarge takes a deep breath and then exhales.

\*\*\*

The Sarge looks at Crystal and then looks at Carlos, "Alright, I'm sending the both of you in. When you go in, do the usual thing. Assess the situation carefully and move slowly. Most importantly and I can't stress this enough, *WATCH* each other's back". "No doubt", Carlos smiles at the Sergeant and then looks at Crystal.

"Let me have the bullhorn", the Sarge tells the officer who is holding it. The officer hands the bullhorn to the Sarge.

The Sarge clears his throat, "Excuse me, everyone. I just want to make a brief announcement. Two of our officers are being sent in and everyone else is on standby. Treat this no differently that any other hostage situation. Everyone keep your ears tuned to me and your eyes tuned to the bank. Let's get those hostages out of there in one piece".

The Sergeant takes the bullhorn down from his mouth and turns to Carlos and Crystal, "Take off your jackets. No weapons. Crystal, you talk to your friend. Maybe we can get this ended smoothly". Crystal looks at the Sarge wide-eyed, "Let's hope".

"If things touch off, give us a signal and we are in there faster than you can blink", the Sarge says this in a deep voice. "I want you to keep this beeper in your shoe", Sarge hands Crystal a small device and she puts it in her sneaker. The Sergeant holds back up the bullhorn to his mouth, "Okay everyone, positions".

Carlos and Crystal take off their jackets and hand them to the other officers. Who would have thought their first *DATE* together would be like this...

Carlos looks at Crystal, "Don't worry. When this is all over, I'll treat you to a sundae". He cracks a smile.

"Oh, you pick a time like this to have jokes", Crystal has a smirk on her face. "There's no time like the present. Alright, let's roll". Carlos and Crystal move swiftly towards the entrance of the bank. Carlos knocks on the door three times and they wait to see if anyone opens the door.

The door opens slowly...it is one of the suspects. Crystal and Carlos walk in slowly. "Put your arms up", the suspect says in a deep voice. Carlos and Crystal slowly put their arms up and the suspect frisk them one at a time. There is another suspect pointing a gun at them.

Crystal slowly scans the bank with her eyes looking around to see if there is anything unusual and counts the hostages. She counts 20 hostages and sees that they are being watched over by another suspect, who is holding a machine gun. After the suspect frisks them, the gunman looks at Crystal strangely and then raises his eyebrows, "Crystal?".

"Raymond?", Crystal's facial expression does **NOT** look amused. "DAMN!", Raymond says this out loud. Carlos wants to smile, but he is saying to himself—**BOY, ARE YOU IN TROUBLE NOW**.

Carlos keeps a straight face. Crystal puts her hand on her hip, "Raymond, what are you doing?. You know this is *NOT* the way to get money. There is something called jobs, Raymond".

Raymond looks up at the ceiling and blows air out of his mouth. Carlos interjects, "Listen while the both of you talk, I'm going to check on the hostages".

Carlos walks over to where the other suspect is. The suspect sees Carlos coming towards him and points his gun in his face, "Step back. Where the hell do you think you're going?!". "I'm unarmed. I'm just here to check on the hostages", Carlos holds up his hands in the air. Raymond shouts over to his friend, "Yo, Breeze. It's cool. Just let him lookover the customers". "Don't tr-tr-try anything stu-stu-stupid", the suspect says with a stutter as he steps back and allows Carlos to check the customers.

Carlos whispers to the customers, "Don't worry. We are going to get all of you out of here. Just be patient". Carlos winks at the customers. Some of the customers are crying, one man is sweating profusely and when Carlos looks around, he notices there are three children. Carlos looks back over at Crystal and nods his head letting her know that the customers are okay.

***

Crystal wastes no time getting under Raymond's skin, "Raymond, why are you doing this?. You know if your mother knew what you was doing right now, she would strangle you just like I'm about to".

"Don't worry, she won't know…she's dead. She died last month", Raymond puts his head down.

Crystal moves closer to Raymond, puts her arms around him and whispers in his ear, "I'm sorry". He embraces her with his free hand (the other hand is holding a gun).

Crystal looks at him, "I just saw your mother a few months ago. I could tell she wasn't well, but she was in good spirits. What happened?".

"She died of breast cancer", Raymond says calmly. "I didn't realize she was that sick". "Yeah, she always looked beautiful, well kept. I don't think anybody knew. My mother had a lot of dignity". "She sure did", Crystal smiles at Raymond.

"Where's your father?". "My father and I don't get along. It was too much to bare staying in that apartment, so he moved away and took my three sisters with him". Crystal shakes her head, "So, who are you staying with?. Are you staying with relatives?".

"No. Everybody lives far…in other states", Raymond says sadly. Crystal stars to ponder, "I think I can be of help. But, you are going to have to trust me".

"My homeboys are not going to be happy, if I skip out on them", Raymond says while raising his eyebrows. Crystal responds quickly, "Listen, this is not about *your* homeys. This is about **YOUR** life, you understand. I know your mother must be rolling around in her grave, because I know she is watching you. Your mother raised you better than that. Don't get me wrong, we all are going to make mistakes. But, the whole idea is not to allow the mistakes to turn into a life long problem. I don't even want to know how you got wrapped up in this mess. The thing now is to get you out of it for good. The only thing I am asking you to do is to cooperate. You think you can do that?".

Raymond scratches his head and sighs, "I…I don't know". Crystal leans closer to Raymond, "Listen, you won't have to do any jail time and I will make sure you get start over somewhere else. One thing you do know about me, I always **KEEP** my promises". Raymond nods his head, "True that. Man…alright.

Alright, I'll do it. I didn't want to do this in the first place. I mean…they said that it was going to be easy money".

"Uh-um. We know what happens, when things come *too* easy", Crystal nods her head. "Yeah, I know. Mommy was right. I should have listened", Raymond's eyes start to get watery.

"It's alright. Let's get this situation over with", Crystal whispers to him. "Anything for you, Crystal. We miss you around the way. You're a cool gal", Raymond breaks out a smile. "Well, thank you", Crystal says in a southern slang.

"Now, first things first. You promised to let the hostages go", Crystal gives Raymond a look of confidence. Raymond's face lights up, "No problem. Let me talk to my partner". Raymond is about to walk over to where his buddy, Breeze is. Crystal stops him, "Before you go, may I have the gun first?". "Sure", Raymond hand the gun to Crystal.

"Yo Ray, what are you doing?", the other suspect yells out to him. "Listen, I can't do this. This is not me. I didn't want to do this in the first place. You don't have to do this either". "Yo, Br-br-eeze is not going to be happy about you bo-bo-bouncing out on us". Raymond shrugs his shoulders, "I don't care. This is *MY* life, not Breeze's".

Raymond looks back at Crystal, turns his head and proceeds to walk over to where Breeze is. Carlos looks at him and then at Crystal. Crystal is holds up the gun and she is smiling. Carlos nods in approval. Raymond walks up to Breeze, "Yo Breeze. Can we let *ALL* of the hostages go?". Breeze looks at him, "No. That was not the agreement. Yo, where is your gun?".

Raymond looks down, then back up right into his face, "I don't want to do this. This ain't right. You don't have to do this. Let's shut this down".

***

Breeze shouts, "*HELL NO!*. Who made you the ring leader. *YOU DO WHAT I SAY!*. I saw you hugging her. I don't care if you know her. I came to get *MINE* and I ain't leaving without it. *NOBODY'S LEAVING!!!*", he cocks his gun. Some of the hostages shriek. Carlos looks at Breeze intensely.

"Yo Breeze, chill. Just chill", Raymond puts his hand up. "No, *YOU* chill", Breeze shoots the gun off into the air. The hostages scream and Raymond tells them to quiet down. Crystal runs over to the front door, before the cops decide to rush in.

She opens the door, takes a white handkerchief out of her pocket and waves it in the air before she steps outside, "Don't worry. We've got it under control. Stand down". She looks at the Sarge and nods her head. The Sarge gets on the bullhorn,

"Everybody stand down!. You only go on *MY* signal". All of the officers hold their positions and Crystal goes back inside the bank.

Carlos talks to the suspect, Breeze, "Listen, why don't you be smart like your friend and let the hostages go". Breeze moves closer to Carlos's face, "Why don't *YOU* be smart and keep your mouth shut!". Carlos pauses, then pretends that one of the hostages is about to make a move by making a gesture with his hand, "No, don't move!".

As the suspect turns his head to see what is going on behind him, Carlos grabs the gun and punches the suspect in the face. The suspect, Breeze hits the ground so hard that the hostages gasp. Carlos hands Raymond the gun and while the suspect is on the ground, he binds the suspect's wrists with plastic handcuffs that were hidden inside the back of his pants.

"Damn...you sucker punched me", Breeze says while slurring his words. Carlos responds, "Yeah. That's what happens, when you're not paying attention." Crystal looks over to see what has happened. Carlos looks over at Crystal and gives her a 'thumbs up'.

The other suspect is looking at what just happened to his buddy, Breeze and then looks at Crystal, "This don't look good. I don't want to die". "You're not going to. You saw what happened to your homey. That's what happens, when you don't do the right thing. And even *if* you thought of this yourself, it's not the way to go". Crystal holds out her hand and the suspect gives her his gun. Crystal smiles back, "Don't worry. I'm going to help you, okay?". "Yeah", the suspect says softly.

Crystal opens the front door, steps outside and gives a signal to the

Sarge for the rest of the officers to come into the bank. The Sarge holds up the bullhorn, "Alright, those up front move in now!. Those of you in the middle, keep your post in front of the bank and the rest follow me".

The Sergeant proceeds to walk towards the bank. As the Sergeant and officers enter the bank, Crystal hands one of the officers the guns. Crystal turns to the Sarge, "Sarge, this young man is one of the suspects. He didn't give us any trouble. I told him we would help him". "You did, uh?", the Sarge raises his eyebrows at Crystal. "Yes, sir", Crystal smiles back.

The suspect has his head down. The Sarge stands in front of him, "Young man. Don't you know you should look a person in the eye, when he or she is talking to you?". The suspect looks up quickly, "Yes, s-s-sir". "Do you know *HOW* serious this was and how serious this could have turned out?", the Sarge says in a deep voice. "Yes sir. I…I'm sorry, sir", the suspect lowers his head again. "It's alright, son. You did the right thing. Just remember that. Don't worry, we are going to help you. Okay?", the Sarge puts his hand on the suspect's shoulder.

"Okay", the suspect looks up at the Sarge and cracks a little smile. "Take this young man in", the Sarge hands the suspect over to two other officers and they take him away.

\*\*\*

Crystal goes over to where Carlos, Raymond and the other suspect are. "Raymond, where is your other friend?". "They are downstairs emptying out the vault". "They?", Carlos says unexpectantly. "Yeah, there are two guys downstairs".

"Listen Raymond, I'm going to do all that I can for you. But for right now, you are going to be handcuffed and taken in for processing. Don't be frightened. I will take care of everything, when I get back to the precinct. Okay?", Crystal puts her arm around his shoulder. Raymond looks at her somberly, "Okay".

Crystal sees the Sarge walking towards them. "Sarge, this is the young man I told you about. He is a good kid. He really is. He just made a bad decision". "Well, I hope he learned his lesson", the Sarge looks at Raymond straight in the eyes.

"Yes sir, I have. I will *NEVER* do this again. Believe me. I'm going back to school". "That sounds like a plan to me", the Sarge pats Raymond on the back.

"Sarge, he's all yours. There are actually *two* more suspects, instead of one and they are downstairs emptying out the vault", Crystal says quickly. "Well, you and Carlos go handle the situation and we'll take it from here". Crystal puts her hand on Raymond's chin, "I'll see you later". Raymond smiles back.

***

The officers round up the customers from the bank and escort them outside. The other officers take Breeze, Raymond and the other suspect into custody. When the crowd sees the customers come out of the bank, they start to cheer. But, things are still not over inside the bank.

Crystal and Carlos head for the basement. They move slowly and as they turn the corner, they can hear two people talking. Crystal holds her finger up to her mouth for Carlos not to say anything. She mouths to Carlos that they will approach the suspects on the count of three. Crystal holds up her hand and counts three with her fingers, one…two…three.

They step out in view, but the suspects have their backs turned putting money from the vault into bags. Carlos startles them, "Woo-woo, Avon calling". Both the suspects *JUMP* and turn around dropping the bags of money.

"Where in the hell did ya'll come from?", one of the suspect's says in a high pitched voice. "Now if I were you, I would hand over the bags and come quietly", Crystal crosses her arms. "You heard the lady. Make it easy on yourself and nobody gets hurt", Carlos says firmly.

The suspects look at each other, they pick up the bags of money off of the floor and then all of a sudden **THROW** the bags of money at Crystal and Carlos. The suspects take off running.

"Now, that was not nice", Carlos says angrily. Carlos and Crystal take off running after them. Carlos corners one of the suspects, who throws a punch and Carlos ducks causing the suspect to go *SPINNING* in a circle. Carlos sweeps the suspect's leg and he goes **CRASHING** to the ground. "Ooooo, I know that hurt", Carlos apprehends the suspect.

Crystal is still running after the other suspect. "You're making this hard for yourself. **STOP!**", Crystal yells out to the suspect. "Only chickens run", Crystal mocks the suspect.

All of a sudden, the suspect stops and turns around, "Who the *hell* you calling a chicken?". Crystal raises her eyebrows, "You". "Alright. We'll see who's a chicken, bitch", the suspect raises his fists. "Oh, now that's not nice. I see you need to be taught some manners", Crystal says sarcastically. She keeps her stance as the suspect move back and forth.

Crystal and the suspect start fighting. The suspect starts doing martial arts. "Oh, I see you're related to Bruce Lee. So am I", Crystal says with a smirk on her face. Crystal blocks the suspect's punches and ducks his kicks. As the suspect is about to kick Crystal, Crystal **kicks** the suspect's inner thigh of his other leg and the suspect *hits* the ground. Crystal hovers over the suspect and punches him in the face, ***STUNNING*** him. Crystal flips him over and handcuffs him. "Who's the *bitch* now", Crystal says firmly. The suspect moans.

Crystal picks up the suspect and takes him outside the bank. She hands the suspect over to one of the officers and meets up with Carlos. "Did he give you a *hard* time?", Carlos says with a smirk on his face. Crystal turns up her lip, "What do *you* think". They both start laughing. Crystal looks over at Raymond, "I have to make sure Raymond gets a second chance. I have to find out how far he has gotten in school and try to contact some of his relatives to see where he can stay".

"That will be good", Carlos nods his head in approval. The Sergeant walks over to Crystal and Carlos, "Great job, guys. I mean, madam". "Thank you, thank you", Crystal smiles back.

"All in a day's work", Carlos shakes the Sarge's hand. "I'll see you back at the precinct", the Sarge turns around and is about to walk away, when Crystal *grabs* him by the arm.

"Listen Sarge. When we get back to the precinct, I need to talk to you about Raymond. He's going to need some help getting back on the right track". "Got caught up with the wrong people?", the Sarge says with concern. "Yeah, but there's a lot *more* to it". "No problem. Anything for you", he winks at Crystal. "Thanks, Sarge".

Crystal walks back over to Carlos, "Well, I guess we're done here. I'm glad everything turned out for the good". "I am, too. Well, let's hit the road. I'm sure another adventure awaits us", Carlos says humorously. Carlos and Crystal walk to their car, get in and take off.

The day has passed quickly and **WHAT** a first day. Crystal got to do what she loves doing everyday—helping others. But, today she got to help a young man whom she *knew*—it's a **SMALL** world. Crystal sometimes *switches* her hats and today she put on her Social Worker hat. As for Carlos, he makes his job so much easier by using his sense of humor. It definitely *helps* the day go faster.

\*\*\*

Evening time has arrived and they are getting ready to go off duty. Carlos is in the locker room along with some of his other co-workers; including his friend, Ramone. "So, how was your first day with Crystal?". "It was good. As good as can be expected. Besides being beautiful, she is a *GOOD* cop", Carlos smiles. "I can agree with you on that. So, when are you going to ask her out?", Ramone says quickly as he grabs his bag and is heading out the door.

Carlos follows him, "What's the rush?. I don't want to spoil the moment. It's not good to be pushy". "You better not take too long. There maybe other guys waiting to *snatch* up that pretty mermaid". "Why, are **YOU** one of them?", Carlos gives Ramone a serious look. "No, my friend. I've got enough in my fish bowl", he puts his hand up. "You're not kidding", Carlos laughs in his face. "Oh, you're funny", Ramone hits him on the back of the head.

They see Crystal walking down the hall and Carlos calls out to her, "Hey, Crystal?". Crystal turns around and sees Carlos and Ramone walking towards her. She stops, 'Hey, guys".

"You're checking out for the night?", Carlos pats her on the shoulder. Crystal nods her head, "Yes. I think we've had enough *excitement* for one day". "True. Listen, would you like to go and get something to eat?", Carlos asks softly.

Ramone raises his eyebrows so *HIGH* that they look like they are about to touch the ceiling of the precinct.

"No, I'm not really hungry. But…I'll take a rain check", she smiles back at Carlos. Carlos is thinking—**I WAS JUST KNOCKED DOWN, BUT I'M NOT DEFEATED.** Carlos moves closer to Crystal, "I'm going to hold you to that". "You do that", Crystal says softly. "You don't mind, if I walk you to your car?". "Of course I do", Crystal says in a serious tone. Both Carlos and Ramone look at her. Crystal then has a smirk on her face, "Just kidding. Sure you can. Ramone, you have a good night". "Have a good night, Crystal", Ramone holds his composure, until Crystal turns around and walks towards the front door.

Ramone slaps Carlos a 'five', "Man, I was worried for a minute. I thought she wasn't going to give you any play".

"I'm not trying to run up on her. I like her a lot and I want to take things slow". "Well, you go ahead, Franklin" (referring to Franklin the turtle), Ramone cracks a smile.

"Good night, Mr. Ramone", Carlos says this in a thick latin accent. "I can at least walk you out to your date", Ramone puts his arm around Carlos's shoulder as they walk out the door.

Crystal is standing outside waiting for Carlos. She sees Carlos and Ramone come out of the precinct. "My car is over there", she points to her car. "Cool", Carlos gives Ramone a handshake and Ramone goes on his way.

"I'm sure you're going to get a good night sleep", Carlos walks closely to Crystal. "I'm going to go by my parent's house and spend a few hours. They are re-painting the inside of their house". "That's nice. Well, let me know if you need an extra set of hands", Carlos has a *BIG* koolaid smile on his face.

"Well, that's mighty nice of you to offer. I'll keep that in mind. Thanks for walking me to my car. You get home safely and…have a good night". "You're welcome, Crystal. You have a good night, too", he walks away in slow motion.

# *two*

━━━━━━━━━━━━━━━━━━━━━━━

Carlos didn't quite get a home run, but at least he got to first base. Just smelling the *SWEET* scent of Crystal is enough for Carlos to savor for the rest of his life. Well, maybe not for the rest of his life...how about a day.

It's a beautiful morning and Carlos is looking forward to another day with Crystal. He's had his shower and is smelling nice; *especially* nice for Crystal. He puts on his clothes and heads downstairs to have breakfast with his parents. His mother, Carmen is in the kitchen preparing breakfast.

"Good morning, mama", Carlos kisses his mother on the cheek. "Good morning, Carlito", she is cooking plantains in a frying pan. She kisses her son on the cheek. Carlos goes to the table and sits with his father, Carlos Sr., "Good morning, son. How are things going?". "Things are going **GREAT!**', he says this with a *BIG* koolaid smile on his face.

His father looks at him, "So, what's up with the koolaid smile?". Carlos looks at his father and tries to wipe the smile from his face. Carmen puts the rest of the food on the table and sits down. "Well pop, I met a nice woman".

"It's about time. I was wondering when you were going to make me a grandfather". "Whoa pop, not so fast. I mean, I've known her for a while now". Carmen smiles, "That's nice. What's her name?".

"Her name is Crystal", Carlos takes some plantains and put them on his plate. "That's a pretty name. Let's see; Crystal and Carlos sitting in a tree, K..I..S..S..I..N..G" (everyone starts laughing). "Okay, ma", Carlos shakes his head and starts to blush.

Carlos Sr. clears his throat, "It doesn't sound Cuban?". Carmen looks at her husband, "Oh boy, here we go". Carlos cuts his eyes at his father, "She's not. That's not important to me". His father snaps back, "It's important to *ME*".

Carmen cuts her eyes at her husband, "Carlos?". "Pop, why are you so hung up on this Cuban pride?. She's a beautiful person and woman". Carmen swallows her juice, "I'm sure she is. Why don't you invite her over for dinner on Sunday". "That will be great. Thanks, ma", he says happily.

His father quickly responds, "So, how long have you known this young lady?". "We've worked together at the same precinct for the past six years. We speak to each other all the time.

We just became partners yesterday. She's a good cop and a caring person. She also has a sense of humor and pop, you always said that was important".

***

"Yes, I did say that. How about her family?". "Crystal's parents have been married for the past 25 years and she has nine brothers and sisters". "That's wonderful. That means we are going to have a *BIG* wedding", Carmen puts her hands up in the air. "Ma", Carlos bashfully shakes his head.

His father wipes his mouth with a napkin, "So, you couldn't find a nice Cuban woman, uh?". Carlos turns his head away from his father without saying a word and looks at his mother, "So ma, what time do you want Crystal over for dinner?".

"Let's see. Six o'clock will be fine. I'm going to cook up a special dinner for her".

Her husband snaps back, "You mean US". Carmen moves closer to her husband's face, "No, you are going to eat at McDonald's". Her husband gives her a funny look. "You know, I need to find out from Crystal if she is free on Sunday. Ma, I've got to get to work. I'll see tonight", Carlos gets up from the table and kisses his mother on the cheek.

"Bye pop", he pats his father on the back. "Have a safe day, son". Carlos grabs his jacket and leaves the house, looking forward to seeing Crystal.

Carmen starts to clear the table; while giving her husband a piece of her mind, "*YOU* have got to stop this. You can't judge people you have not met". "I can judge whomever I want. She is welcomed here for dinner, but she will *NOT* be welcomed into *THIS* family".

"You're such a stubborn jackass", Carmen walks away from him and says something in Spanish under her breath. "I heard that!", her husband says loudly.

Is what Carlos Jr. facing anything new?... not really. It is a common thread that takes place in so many families. Ignorance, fear, call it what you will. Carmen and Carlos Jr. have had to *LIVE* with a person they love who doesn't like people for who they are. They've decided to tolerate the 'curse' that their father and husband has lived with most of his life. Let's hope that some of that love can convince Carlos Sr. to be more *'loving'* to others.

***

Carlos and Crystal are on patrol. Carlos is doing the honors again today by chauffeuring Crystal. Carlos is so excited that his mother has invited Crystal over for dinner and holding is breath for a YES from Crystal.

"So Crystal, have you ever eaten Cuban food?". "Can't say that I have", she reaches in the glove compartment of the car and pulls out some papers. Carlos smiles, "Good…would you like to have dinner this Sunday at my parent's home?".

Crystal looks over at him, "Hmmm. Does your mom cook good?".

"WHAT!. Your mouth will water after you take the first bite. I'm not just saying that, because she's my mom".

"Uh, huh. Well, I would love to come to your parent's home for dinner. Even if your mother wasn't a good cook, I would still come", Crystal smiles back. "THAT'S GREAT!",

Carlos yells out and then he realizes his tone. "Really…great", he's cracking that koolaid smile, again.

"Oh Carlos, don't forget. I need to go by and see how Raymond is doing. I already spoke to the Sarge and he said it was okay for us to go". Carlos asks Crystal for directions on how to get to Long Island, where Raymond is staying.

After traveling for about an hour, Crystal and Carlos arrive to where Raymond is staying. Carlos parks the car in front of the house, they get out and walk up to the house. The house is a beautifully kept two-family home with flowers lining the walkway. One can hear the birds chirping and Crystal was just thinking at that moment how **BLESSED** Raymond was to get out of that madness and go somewhere serene. Crystal hopes that this *second* chance will be the chance that Raymond needs to get his life back on the right track.

Crystal rings the bell and the door opens. "Hi, Raymond", Crystal puts her arms out to give him a hug. "Hey Crystal, how's it going?", he gives her a hug. Raymond sees Carlos and shakes his hand, "Hi sir". "Sir?. I'm not that old. You can call me Carlos. It's cool".

They go inside and everyone sits in the living room. Crystal looks around the livingroom and sees that it is nicely decorated. She then looks back at Raymond, "So, how are you doing?. If you are doing well as this house looks, then you're doing alright".

"I'm doing great. School is going pretty well, too", he gives her a gracious smile. Carlos is glad to hear that,

"That's good. So, do you know what you want to do after you have finished school?".

Raymond folds his hands, "I want to be a doctor. I owe it to my mother. I know I can't bring her back, but maybe I can help save other people". Crystal looks at him like a proud mother, "Oh, I'm really proud of you. I know the transition hasn't been easy for you, but I'm glad that you didn't choke up. You could've said no and stayed with your homeboys (Crystal raises her eyebrows). But, I'm glad and I know your mother would have been glad, too. Is anybody home?".

"No. My cousins went out. They will be back later. Would you like something to drink?", Raymond stands up.

"No Raymond, I'm good", Crystal waves her hand for Raymond to sit back down. Carlos leans forward, "Listen, I'm glad you're staying focused. We had a talk with the Sarge and he said that as long as you stay out of trouble, you case will be closed next year".

"That'll be great. Believe me after that last experience, you won't have to worry about me getting into trouble, again". Crystal puts her arm around Raymond, "I'm going to help you get into medical school, when you are ready. To start off, you should go to the library and get a few medical books. You let me know what day next week is good for me to come and pick you up to take you to the library".

"That'll be cool. Thanks for everything, Crystal", he hugs her. "You are so welcome". Carlos looks at his watch, "Crystal, we better get going. We have to make our rounds. Raymond, take care of yourself and I'll see you at your graduation". Carlos stands up and so does Raymond. They give each other a hug. "And if you need to have a man-to man talk, just give me a call", Carlos winks at Raymond. "I'll do that", Raymond smiles back at Carlos.

Crystal gets up from the sofa and they walk towards the front door. Raymond opens the door, "Oh Carlos, take care of my lady". "Oh, don't worry. I've always got her back", Carlos gives him a handshake. "Alright Raymond, you be good and we love you", she smiles at him. Raymond's eyes start to get watery as Crystal and Carlos walk back to their car.

\*\*\*

They get into their car and drive off. "I'm so happy that he's doing well. I know his mother is smiling", Crystal nods her head. "Well, that's what happens when you have an *angel* watching over you", Carlos looks at Crystal and smiles.

"So, what were we talking about…oh yeah, Sunday. I have to pick out something nice to wear", Crystal starts humming a song. "Don't worry. I'll make a good impression", she raises her eyebrows at Carlos. "Oh, I'm not worried. I know you *will* look beautiful", he raises his eyebrows back at her.

# *three*

---

When it comes to that saying, "A little intervention goes a long way", that definitely worked for Raymond. Raymond may be on his way to being someone others can reach out to for help, just like he reached out for help.

Time does not stand still, because Sunday evening has arrived. Crystal is looking and smelling sweet for her **BIG** night. Oh boy…this can be compared to a virgin losing his/her virginity, a couple on their honeymoon or a couple's first kiss. Oh yes…meeting someone's parents for the **FIRST** time is a *BIG* deal.

Crystal checks her watch as she pulls up to Carlos's house. It is exactly 5:55pm. She has five whole minutes, before she rings the bell to his parent's home. She gets out of the car and walks up to the door. She looks at her watch and as 5:59pm approaches, she rings the doorbell.

***

The door opens and it is Carlos (they both have those koolaid smiles on their faces). "You look beautiful", Carlos says slowly. "Thank you…and may I say you're looking rather spiffy yourself", she responds. "Come in", Carlos steps to the side, so Crystal cam come into the house.

Carlos takes her purse and sees that she is holding a bouquet of flowers, "Those are for me?". "No. They are for your mom". "Ah, nice touch", Carlos says jokingly.

Carlos escorts Crystal into the livingroom to meet his parents. Carmen and Carlos Sr. see Crystal walking into the livingroom with Carlos and they both get up from the couch.

"Mom, dad, this is Crystal. Crystal, this is my mother, Carmen". Carmen extends her hand to Crystal, "It is a pleasure to finally meet you, Crystal". Crystal shakes her hand, "It's a pleasure to meet you, too. Here, these are for you". Crystal hands Carmen the bouquet of flowers. "For me?. That is so sweet of you. Thank you. Please, come sit".

Carlos Sr. extends his hand to Crystal, "Hi, I'm Carlos Sr.". "It is nice to meet you, sir", Crystal shakes his hand and sits on the couch.

***

Carlos sits next to Crystal and his father sits over in a side chair. "I'm going to go and put these flowers in some water. I'll be right back", Carmen goes into the kitchen.

Carlos Sr. clears his throat, "The flowers are beautiful. So, my son tells me you're his partner at the precinct". "Yes. We've been working together for about a week now, but we've known each other for six years. It's going pretty well so far. He's very protective of me".

"I'm not surprised. My son is a good cop. It runs in the family blood". Carmen comes out of the kitchen with the flowers in a vase and sets the vase on a side table. Carmen goes over to the couch and sits next to Crystal, "My son has told us so much about you. So far everything is true. You are beautiful".

Crystal becomes bashful, "Please. You're going to make me blush". "So Crystal, why did you decide to become a cop?", Carmen leans forward. "I've always liked the challenge of being an officer and helping people". "Don't you ever feel scared about being confronted by someone with a gun?", Carmen says with concern. Crystal then pauses for a moment, "I've gotten use to it over the years". "I don't know. I just think women should not be doing that type of work. It is too dangerous", Carmen folds her arms.

*** 

Carlos reassures his mother, "Ma, Crystal's a tough lady. She can take care of herself". Carlos smiles at Crystal and puts his arm around her.

Carlos Sr. decides to put his two cents in, "So Crystal, what do your parents do?".

"My father is a self-employed accountant and my mother is a retired engineer". Carlos Sr. raises his eyebrows, "Productive people". Carlos looks at his father as if to say—**DON'T EVEN THINK OF IT!**.

Carmen notices the sarcasm from her husband and gets up from the couch, "Okay everyone, the food is ready. Let's all go into the diningroom". Carlos *jumps* up from the couch, "No time is better than the present. Crystal, shall we". Carlos takes her hand as she gets up and escorts her to the diningroom.

Carlos and Crystal are walking behind Carlos's father. Carlos whispers in Crystal's ear, "Don't pay my father any mind. He has issues". Crystal looks at Carlos, "Oh, I see". Everyone sits down at the table. Crystal is sitting next to Carlos and Carmen is sitting next to her husband.

"Well Crystal, I hope you like to eat, because I made *plenty* of food and there will be plenty to take home with you", she says joyfully. "Great. I don't have to cook for the next few days", Crystal chuckles. Carmen and Carlos laugh, Carlos's father just puts a fake smile on his face. Carlos looks at his father *cautiously*.

Carlos says grace and Carmen starts sharing out the food. Everyone starts eating. Crystal takes a few bites of the food and swallows, "This is delicious, Mrs. Ruiz". "Thank you. I'm glad you like it and please, call me Carmen. Eat up and make sure you leave room for dessert". Carlos makes eye contact with his father from time to time and his father shows *disgust* in his eyes.

The evening is almost gone and they have finished their dinner. Carmen starts clearing the table, but Carlos takes the dishes out of her hand, "Ma, I got this. You go and rest. You did enough work for one day". Crystal steps in, "That's right, we've got it. By the way, the food was heavenly. Especially, the fish". "I made it especially for you. Carlos told me you loved fish". "Oh, did he?", Crystal looks at Carlos with a smirk on her face. Carlos has that koolaid smile on his face. Crystal and Carlos finish clearing the table and go into the kitchen to wash the dishes.

Carmen goes and sits on the couch next to her husband, "Well, I get treated like a queen today". "You get treated like a queen everyday", Carlos Sr. kisses his wife on the lips. "I don't know about that", Carmen rolls her eyes at him. Carmen and Carlos Sr. can hear Crystal and Carlos laughing from the kitchen.

Carlos Sr. looks at his wife, "So, what do you think of Crystal?". "She seems very nice. She's beautiful, intelligent and well-mannered. I hear wedding bells", Carmen taps her chin with her finger. "Don't break open the champagne just yet. We have not met the rest of the family", her husband responds sarcastically. "Why are you looking for problems?. You should be happy your son has found someone who makes him happy". "Yeah, we'll see", Carlos Sr. shakes his head.

Crystal and Carlos come out of the kitchen and join his mother and father in the livingroom. Carlos sits in the side chair and Crystal sits next to Carlos's father.

Carlos Sr. wastes no time, "Well, Carlos told us that you have a big family. Does everybody work?". Crystal looks at him strangely, "Excuse me?". Carmen taps her husband's arm with her arm and Carlos Jr. looks up at the ceiling as if to say—**NO HE DIDN'T!.**

"Pop!", Carlos quickly replies. Crystal interjects, "Why do you ask?". "Well, I know how hard it is for people to find jobs", Carlos Sr. keeps his eyes *glued* on Crystal. Carlos is looking at his mother and vice versa. Crystal sticks it back to Carlos's father, "Well if that's the case, then my family doesn't have any problems in that area".

\*\*\*

Carlos is nodding his head at his father as if to say—**RIGHT BACK AT YOU!**. Carlos starts talking, "Oh ma, remember that dish you made the other night?. Can you make it one day this week?. I want Crystal to try it". Carmen smiles, "Oh sure, I'll make it for her. So Crystal, would you like to get married someday?". "Yes, I would. I hope to find the right man. It's pretty hard these days". "I know what you mean…and do you want a big wedding?".

Her husband turns his head and looks at her as if to say-**WHAT IN THE HELL ARE YOU THINKING!**. "Yes, I do", Crystal looks at Carlos. Carlos has a 'Garfield the cat' smile on his face. But guess who's not smiling?. Crystal continues on, "I have a big family". Carlos Sr. jumps in, "Can you *AFFORD* a big wedding?".

"**POP!**", Carlos raises his voice. Crystal puts her hand up, "No, Carlos. It's okay. I got this. Mr. Ruiz, do you have a problem with uh…African-American people?". Carlos Sr. sits up straight, "As a matter of fact, *I do*". "**POP!**", Carlos shouts. Carlos's father raises his voice, "NO. She opened up the book, so let her read me".

This is definitely *NOT* what Crystal had in mind in reference to— MEETING THE PARENTS.

\*\*\*

Crystal slowly gets up and stands right in front of Carlos's father, because he is about to get **READ,** "First of all, you are the one who opened the book that only **YOU** was reading. Secondly Mr. Ruiz, I don't know what your personal problems are and *whom* they are with, but you just met me and obviously *you* have some unresolved issues in which you should seek counseling.

Carlos Sr. jumps up, "Excuse me young lady, but you are in **MY** house!". Carmen gets up and steps in front of her husband, "That's enough. First of all, this is *OUR* house. Secondly, Crystal is a guest in this house". Carmen turns to Crystal, "Crystal, I want to apologize on behalf of my prejudice husband". "Don't apologize", Carlos's father says this in a thick Cuban accent.

Carlos walks over to Crystal, "Crystal, do you want me to take you home?". "Yes, please. Actually, you can walk me outside". Carmen grabs Crystal's hand, "Please Crystal, don't leave. I mean...I understand if you have to". "I'm sorry, Mrs. Ruiz". "Please, call me Carmen", she squeezes Crystal's hand. Crystal smiles at Carmen, "Maybe we can go shopping, sometimes". "That'll be nice. Thank you for coming", Carmen hugs Crystal. "It was my pleasure", Crystal embraces Carmen.

Crystal walks past Carlos's father like he didn't exist. Carlos gets her purse and walks her outside.

Steam is coming out of Carmen's ears as she turns around to face her husband, **"WHAT IN THE HELL IS WRONG WITH YOU?!.** Why do you have to mess up things for our son?". The wind from her breath was *so strong* that she causes her husband's mustache hairs to stand on end. "I'm thinking about what is *BEST* for this family". **"NO!.** You are *ONLY* thinking about yourself", Carmen walks away and says something in Spanish. "Good night to you, too", her husband waves her off with his hand.

*Pride* is not just a strong word, but a negative attribute. It is an attribute that does not come with a lot of benefits. Carlos Sr. may be finding this out the *HARD* way. Carlos knew his father's views were strong, but he didn't think that he would *infringe* them on **HIS** life. Choice is definitely one of life's complex ingredients and from this point on, Carlos will be making more difficult ones.

Carlos tries to console Crystal, "Crystal, I am so sorry. I didn't expect my father to act that way". Crystal is leaning against her car, "I don't blame you. I feel sorry for your father, because he's ignorant". Carlos moves closer to Crystal, "I want to apologize for my father's behavior". "You've lived with your father all of your life and you never knew he was like that?".

Carlos sighs, "Actually…I did. But that's *his* problem. I'm not going to let him ruin my life and not this evening. I would like to make it up to you. What's that saying, (Carlos looks up at the sky and then looks at Crystal) the night is still young". Crystal strokes Carlos's face with her hand, "It is, it is. So, what do you have in mind?". "Well, I know a nice restaurant that has a jukebox that plays oldies", Carlos nods his head.

Crystal's face slowly breaks into a smile, "I'd like that. I'm glad you're not like your father". "So am I. Are you ready, madam?", he opens the car door. "I am, sir", she gets in the passenger seat. Carlos gets in the driver's seat, she hands him the keys, he starts up the car and takes off.

Things just went from sour to *sweet* and yes…the night is *still* young.

They arrive downtown and Carlos drives around, until he finds a parking space. They get out and stroll down the Boulevard.

*** 

They see a couple of nice restaurants and Carlos stops in front of one of them, "This is the place. Shall we?", Carlos holds out his arm. "We shall", Crystal puts her hand over his arm and they walk into the restaurant. There are a few patrons still dining, but it's not too crowded. They walk up to the Maitre'd.

"A table for two", Carlos tells the man. "Surely, please follow me", the man escorts them to a table near the window. "Thank you", Carlos puts some money in the man's hand. He kindly replies, "Thank you".

Carlos pulls out a chair for Crystal, so she can sit down. "Why, thank you", she says in a southern voice as she sits. "You are quite welcome", Carlos walks back over to the other seat and sits down. "I am glad we were able to get a table with a nice view", Crystal looks out the window. "Yeah, it is a beautiful night", Carlos gazes into Crystal's eyes.

"I'm sorry again for what happened at the house", Carlos says apologetically. "Let's forget about it for right now. This is OUR time. I just want to enjoy the rest of the evening with you", Crystal places her hand on top of Carlos's hand. Carlos smiles back, "Would you like dessert?". "Sure, that sounds good", Crystal says softly.

\*\*\*

Carlos waves over the waiter and asks him to bring a menu. After the waiter leaves, Crystal and Carlos hold each other's hand. "I'm not going to eat too much dessert", Carlos says softly. "Why, are you on a diet?", Crystal looks at Carlos strangely. "No. I'm looking forward to getting some sugar later", he puts that koolaid smile on his face. Crystal shakes her head, "Oh, oh. Is this the Carlos I haven't met yet?". "I hope not", he raises his eyebrows at her and she laughs.

Time is standing still and it could not have happened at a better time. In the background, there is a jazz song playing and Crystal has her ears tuned to the music. "I know that song". "Really, would you like to dance?", Carlos extends his hand to Crystal. Crystal puts her hand in his and they walk to the middle of the room, which is a dance floor.
There is no one else there, but them. As far as Crystal and Carlos were concerned, they were the only two people in the restaurant. They move in closer to one another; Crystal is smelling the scent of Carlos' sweet body and Carlos is enjoying the sweet scent of Crystal's *heavenly* body. They look into each other's eyes as they slowly dance. Crystal places one hand on Carlos's back and the other hand in his hand. Carlos has his other hand around Crystal's waist.

\*\*\*

"So, do you do this often?", Crystal says softly. "Not really", Carlos is eye to eye with Crystal; not missing a beat. "You could have fooled me", she gives him a little grin. This moment feels so right for Crystal and Carlos. They are drawn to each other like humming birds and their lips are drawn together like a magnet as they move in closer for a passionate kiss. **WOW!**, this is what *SWEET* is.
As they pull back from their kiss, the fireworks are going off at ***FULL***

blast. Crystal sighs, "That was nice". "I hope we can do this again", Carlos says in a low voice. "Don't worry, we will".

Crystal starts to hum the song that is playing and they continue to dance *slowly* cheek to cheek. Every now and then glancing into each other's eyes. In their minds, this is just the beginning of something **GREAT**. For Crystal, it has been worth the wait and for Carlos, there is no other woman who can compare to the one that is standing before him.

So as the evening passes and the night comes in, Crystal and Carlos savor their first date. The good and the bad of it. Carlos takes Crystal home and when he arrives home, he calls Crystal just so he can hear *HER* voice. Crystal's phone rings and she answers it, "Hello?". "Hi, beautiful lady", Carlos says sweetly.

"Hey, you got home quickly". "I couldn't wait to get home…just so I could talk to you. Would you like to go on a picnic, next Sunday?", he is looking at his calendar. "Well, let's see. I think I'm available on that day". "*YES!*", he shouts forgetting that he is still on the phone.

"I mean…that's great. Is noon okay?". "That's fine. Is everything okay between you and your dad?". "No. He's such a stubborn man. He can't tell me who to love". "You're right. Especially, if that person loves you", she is smiling.

Carlos is grinning like a kid in a candy store, "So…you love me, uh?". Crystal chuckles, "Yeah, I guess you could say that. Thank you for dinner…and dessert. You'll make a good husband one day". Carlos is on cloud nine and he *doesn't* want to come down. "You get some sleep. Thanks for calling and I'll see you tomorrow". "Sweet dreams, Crystal". "Sweet dreams, Carlos".

As they each hang up their phones, they both realize that they were meant to be together. Was it just a coincidence that they became partners at the precinct?… probably not. Divine intervention definitely had these two beautiful people put together for a reason. To start a journey and finish it…**TOGETHER.**

# *four*

24 hours is definitely not going to be enough time for Carlos to forget what his father did to Crystal. Carlos may want to check his birth certificate to make sure the the name of his father is correct. Unfortunately, Carlos still has to live in the same house with his father.

So as Carlos and his parents sit down to have breakfast, Carlos tries not to have eye contact with his father. Carlos finishes his breakfast quickly and gets up from the table. "Ma, I'll see you tonight", Carlos gives his mother a kiss on the cheek. "You have a good day, son. Oh, tell Crystal I said hello". "I will", Carlos says to her as he heads out the door.

As you can see, he *ONLY* acknowledges his mother. His father grunts under his breath as he chews his food. Carmen takes a sip of her juice and then looks at her husband, "Keep it up. You're going to be a lonely man". She gets up from the table and takes the dishes into the kitchen. Carlos Sr. continues to grunt under his breath.

***

Carlos Sr. may not realize it now, but how he thinks is about to **BLOW** up in his face and it's not only going to affect him.

The day had gone quickly, because Crystal and Carlos are getting off from work. They run into each other in the hallway. Crystal is holding a beautiful bouquet of flowers, "You know, someone left these beautiful flowers in front of my locker this morning. You wouldn't know who could have left them there?".

Carlos has this silly look on his face, "It could have been the flower fairy". Crystal moves closer to his face, "The flower fairy. Uh, uh". "Yeah. He's a pretty popular person", Carlos tries to keep a straight face. Crystal puts her hand on her hip, "How do you know the fairy is a he?". That silly look is still on Carlos's face, "I ran into him, when I was leaving the locker room".

Crystal can't contain herself and neither can Carlos as they both *BURST* out laughing. "I'm really looking forward to Sunday", Crystal rubs Carlos's chin. "So am I. Do you need a ride home?". "Actually, I do. My car was acting up this morning, so I put it in the auto shop". Carlos holds out his arm, "Shall we?". Crystal wraps her hand around his arm, "We shall".

***

They walk out together to his car and they both have those big koolaid smiles on their faces. *AW*, what a perfect opportunity to vibe, alone. I'm sure Carlos is not thinking about his father and neither is Crystal. This is **THEIR** moment.

Carlos arrives to Crystal's apartment and escorts her to her front door. "Would you like something to drink?", Crystal says without hesitation. Carlos responds quickly, "Yes. That would be nice". As Crystal opens the door, she doesn't see the expression on Carlos's face— **HAAPPPYYYYY**…

As Carlos walks into the apartment, he looks around and sees that it is clean, neat and smells lovely. To Carlos; those are some of the qualities to look for, when you're looking for 'wife' material.

"Very nice place", Carlos says as he continues to look around the apartment. "Thank you. I do my best. I love decorating", Crystal places her keys on a hook on the wall. "Let me take your jacket", Crystal gestures to Carlos and Carlos is saying to himself—**WOW, SHE REALLY LIKES ME.** Crystal hangs up her jacket and then his.

"You can have a seat, while I get you something to drink", Crystal goes into the kitchen. Carlos sees that Crystal has an open kitchen and he has a full view of her.

"What would you like to drink?", Crystal asks kindly. "What do you have?". "Well, I have apple juice, cranberry juice, grape juice, ginger ale and tea". Crystal pauses for a moment, "Oh yeah…and water". Carlos chuckles, "Grape juice is fine". Crystal goes into the cabinet and takes out two glasses. She then goes into the refrigerator and gets the grape juice. Carlos *still* has his eyes on Crystal, "So, how long have you been living here?". "I've been living here for about five years. I love this neighborhood", Crystal says while pouring the juice in a glass for Carlos. She then pours juice into her glass. She comes out of the kitchen and hands Carlos his glass of juice. "Thanks", Carlos takes the glass of juice and takes a sip.

Crystal sits closely next to Carlos. As they drink their juice, Crystal looks at Carlos bashfully with a smile on her face. They both put their glasses on the coffee table. Carlos starts twiddling his fingers and Carlos fixes her hair, while she looks at Carlos. You can *hear* crickets as the both of them sit quietly, gazing into each other's eyes.

*** 

Carlos finally breaks the silence, "That's good that you have your own place. Sometimes I wish I had my own place. It's okay, though. I'm saving my money; so when I'm ready to settle down, I can be able to take care of my wife". Crystal nods her head in approval, "That's good planning. Sounds like you're going to be a good hubby. Even if I had a husband who wanted to take care of me, I would still work. I like to keep myself busy".

Carlos is thinking to himself—**SHE'S INDEPENDENT. GOOD QUALITY.** Carlos stops twiddling fingers, "Do you date much?". Crystal turns her body towards Carlos, "No, not really. I've been on a few dates. I have not met anyone that I felt comfortable with...until now".

Crystal lowers her head and Carlos raises his eyebrows as high as they could go. Carlos is saying to himself—**YES!**. "So, you have the hots for me, uh?". Crystal laughs, "I guess you could say that. I find you caring, quite intelligent, funny and...handsome. Oh, maybe I should not have said that. I wouldn't want to swell up your head". "Oh, you got jokes", Carlos says jokingly.

Crystal chuckles, "It's funny. I've been watching you for the past couple of years, but I didn't have the nerve to ask you out". "I thought that was *MY* job", Carlos rubs his chin. "Not really. My thing is if a person likes another person, he or she should let that person know".

Carlos leans forward, "So, why didn't you let me know?". "Because...you beat me to it", Crystal taps Carlos on the nose with her finger. "So, what about you. You date much?". Carlos slowly eases his arm around Crystal's shoulder, "No. I'm particular about the women I date. I've dated a few women, but I haven't hit a spark...until now". Crystal is **BEAMING**. If she cuts the lights off, she would probably *glow* in the dark.

Carlos starts to rub her shoulder, "Since you haven't dated much, you must be out of practice". Crystal looks at him strangely, "Out of practice with what?". Carlos whispers to her, "Kissing". Crystal giggles, "Yeah. It's been a while". "Care for some lessons?", Carlos stares straight into Crystal's eyes. "How long are the lessons for?", Crystal strokes his face with his hand. "For as long as you would like".

Carlos puts his hand on her face and as they lean towards each other, their lips *embrace* into a soft kiss. That kiss continues on and on and on and...well, you've got the idea. My, my, my, ain't love grand.

\*\*\*

Well, that kiss is probably still simmering. When it comes to love, anything is possible. It is a feeling that is indescribable and deep. So deep that nothing and no one can interfere with it. Will their love be **DEEP** enough to withstand the poison that is coming from Carlos's father?... only time will tell.

Sunday has come. Crystal and Carlos are at a park having a picnic. Crystal bought a beautiful blanket for them to sit on and a basket full of goodies. The sun is shining brightly and there is a calm breeze keeping the air cool. Crystal has on a beautiful baby blue summer dress that has flower petals embroidered on it. It just so happens that Carlos wore a baby blue shirt and navy blue khaki pants. Carlos is admiring the flower that Crystal has in her hair and her pretty feet. Crystal is quite impressed by Carlos's manicured feet. I think that would impress any woman, whether she liked the man or not.

Crystal looks up at the sky, "It's a beautiful day". "And you make it more beautiful", Carlos winks at Crystal. He then opens a bottle of sparkling cider. "Oooo, bubbly", Crystal says jokingly. Carlos pours the cider into two wine glasses and gives one of the glasses to Crystal. He puts the bottle of cider down and holds up his glass, "I would like to make a toast. To you and I. May we grow to love one another". "Yes. Absolutely", Crystal agrees as they clink their glasses.

They take a sip of the cider and savor the moment, while rubbing noses like Eskimos. Carlos brought along to the picnic a boombox radio and he puts on a song. Crystal packed some fruit for the picnic and she brought a variety—apples, bananas, grapes and pineapples. Crystal starts with the grapes. She feeds Carlos some grapes, one by one and he returns the favor.

She then picks up an apple; Carlos bites into the apple and slowly chews, while the juices run down his chin.

Crystal picks up a napkin and wipes his chin. She then bites into the apple. Juice from the apple starts to run down her chin and instead of Carlos getting a napkin, he kisses off the juices with his lips—*YUMMY*. After that, she picks up a banana—*MMMMM*. She licks her lips as she slowly peels and I mean...**s l o w l y** peels the banana.

She bites a piece of the banana and chews it. Carlos raises one eyebrow. She takes another bite and he raises *both* eyebrows. The temperature just went **UP!**. *MAN OH MAN*, who says you need to have sex to have an orgasm.

They move closer together and move in for some more *SUGAR*. They move closer and closer and just as they are about to kiss…**BOP!**. A ball comes out of nowhere and hits them on their heads. A little boy about eight years old comes running up to them. "Sorry", the boy says to them. Carlos gives the ball back to the little boy.

Carlos and Crystal look at each other and smile. "Could that be a sign?", Carlos touches Crystal's face. "Yeah. That we should keep our eyes open". They both laugh. They give each other a quick kiss on the lips.

Carlos takes Crystal's hand, "When would you like to get married?". "I don't know. When the time is right. Certain things need to be in place. Why do you ask?". "I was just curious". Crystal rubs Carlos's hand, "I want to make sure that I know the person that I'm marrying first. That's important. No one is perfect, but he has to be secure financially, sound mind and a sincere spirit. And if I do have a wedding, I want to invite people who are very close to me. I would try to keep it small. What about you?".

"I feel the same way. I want to be with someone who is sure of herself, independent, caring, street smart and book smart. Someone who can balance family and work. As far as a wedding, it doesn't matter. Whatever she wants is fine. However, I don't want a huge wedding. Something simple".

Crystal has this look on her face as if a light bulb just went off in her head, "Listen, I have an idea". Carlos looks at her curiously, "What?". "Would you like to go to the beach?".

"That sounds great. When?". She grins, "Now". He's thinking- **SPONTANEOUS. I'M LOVING THIS WOMAN.** Carlos smiles, "Let's go".

\*\*\*

He kisses her on the lips and they start packing up their things. They get everything packed and take it to Carlos's car. Everything is put away in the trunk and she gets in the driver's seat. Again he's thinking—**A WOMAN WHO LIKES TO TAKE THE LEAD SOMETIMES. YEP, SHE'S THE ONE!.**

By the time they reached the beach it is late in the afternoon. Carlos finds a cozy spot, so they can continue where they left off. Crystal had excused herself to go to the ladies room and when she came back, she had a beautiful flower in her hair.

"Waiting for someone?", Crystal looks like a blossoming flower ready to be picked. Carlos is even *more* pleased by her beauty, "You could say that. My, you are definitely a sight for sore eyes. Come join me". Crystal sits as close to Carlos as two people could be. She strokes his face softly.

Carlos sighs, "Would you like to go for a walk?". "I would love to". Carlos gets up, Crystal extends her hand and he pulls her up. Carlos had a smaller radio in the trunk of his car, so he decided to bring it along. He holds the radio in one hand and his other hand is around Crystal's shoulder.

\*\*\*

They start leaving *'footprints in the sand'* as they take their walk on the beach. The waves are crashing against the shore calmly and there are birds flying over head. They could take *this* moment and lock it up in a treasure chest, so they could keep it for a lifetime.

Crystal looks into Carlos's eyes, "Now that I know you love me, I can share the good news with my family. But, how are you going to tell your father?". Carlos pauses for a moment, "I'm sure my father will just be THRILLED. I'm not going to worry about how and what he has to say. I care more about my mom's blessing. The time feels right. I need someone like you in my life".

"Same here. Well I don't know about you, but you are going to have to keep up with me". "Really now. Actually, I think it's the other way around. Come on, don't be a slacker", Carlos starts jogging backwards. Crystal starts chasing after him. Carlos turns around and speeds up, but Crystal catches up with him and he gives her a bear hug.

They walk back to where they left their blanket. Carlos puts the radio down on the blanket and there is a song playing. They start to dance; moving *slowly* together, their bodies *swaying* like the waves of the ocean.

\*\*\*

This is love at it's inception. They are enjoying *their* moment in time. They hope for many more like this. And as the song ends, so as not their love. For that will play on and on and on and…

Carlos has found love and it could not have come at a better time. It feels good and he knows that Crystal is the **ONE.** He's not hesitant about sharing how he feels with his parents. Hmmm, his father just may go deaf after hearing *what* his son has to say. Carlos decides to break the news tomorrow night at dinner. He didn't want to spoil the *wonderful* day he had with Crystal.

Carlos, his mother and father are sitting at the table having dinner. "How is Crystal doing?", his mother says before she takes a sip of water. "She's doing great, ma. Ma, I'm glad you mentioned her. I have something to tell the both of you". His father swallows his food, "I hope it's good news". Carlos puts down his fork, "Oh pop, don't worry. *IT* is. Mom…dad,

I love Crystal and-".

"I knew it!", Carmen jumps in before Carlos could finish his sentence. She is excited, but his father keeps a straight face. Carlos finishes his sentence, "And I'm going to ask her to marry me".

Carmen jumps out of her chair, goes over to Carlos, hugs and kisses him, "Oh my baby. I am so happy for you. I am so happy for me. My baby is going to have babies...grand babies". "Oh ma", Carlos hugs his mother ever so tightly.

His father drops his fork, "So, that's the good news. You're going to marry a-". Carlos interjects quickly in a loud voice, "Just watch your mouth pop!. She has a name". His father raises his voice even louder, **"DON'T YOU RAISE YOUR VOICE AT ME!. THIS IS MY HOUSE!.** You give me respect".

Carlos gets up, **"RESPECT**...respect. You wouldn't know *what* respect was if it came up to you and bit you on the-". His mother interjects, "Carlos!". "You've lost my respect, pop". His father gets up and moves closer to his son's face, "Then leave...**LEAVE!.**

Carmen steps in between the both of them, "No, listen...the both of you. You're both just upset. Let's all sit back down and talk". "No, Carmen. There's nothing to talk about", his father says pridefully. He then looks back at his son, "Get out of my house!". "Fine. I'm leaving", Carlos is nose to nose with his father. "No son, don't leave", his mother says emotionally while holding on tightly to her son's arm.

***

"No ma. I don't want to stay here with a racist bastard". Just as the last syllable comes out of Carlos's mouth; his father raises his hand and like a bat about to hit a baseball, he takes his hand with a *FULL* swing and **SLAPS** Carlos on his face.

The impact was so *GREAT* that he left an imprint of his hand on the left side of Carlos's face and an echo of the slap lingered in the air. Carmen's mouth dropped open and she is in ***SHOCK***. There is dead silence. Carlos looks at his father as if he wants to ***hurt*** him...**REALLY BAD**.

Carmen regains her composure and sounds off to her husband as tears roll down her cheeks, **"WHY DID YOU DO THAT?!. WHAT IS WRONG WITH YOU!".** She starts to cry. Carlos comforts his mother, "Don't cry, ma". He then looks back at his father, "I'm finished with you. You are...no longer...my father!".

He then *SPITS* in front of his father's feet. If anyone knows Cuban culture, that means total disrespect. Carlos loosens his mother's grasp and walks out of the house. His mother yells out, **"CARLOS!"**. Carlos **SLAMS** the door so hard that it causes the walls in the house to vibrate.

Carmen turns slowly and looks at her husband with tears still rolling down her face, "Are you *that* stupid to hit your own grown child...for nothing. You can not tell him *who* to love". She wipes her face with her hands and then brings her voice up a notch, "You're wrong, **YOU'RE WRONG!**. If I did not love you so much, I would leave you. Carlos, you have a lot to think about and when you are ready to talk, you let me know. Because right now, I can't stand the *sight* of you".

She walks out of the room and begins to cry again. Her husband reaches out his hand to her, but she is gone. He **pounds** his fist onto the table, grabs a glass and **smashes** it onto the floor. He then sits down and puts his hands on his head.

The damage has been done. Carlos Sr. has a *LOT* to think about. Not just his family situation, but also his attitude. There is **NO** room for pride. The same pride that flows through his blood could have spilled some blood. Carlos Sr. has a lot to confess. The question for him is **WHEN?**.

Carlos already knew *where* he was headed, when he left his house. So when Crystal's doorbell rang, she wondered who it could have been. She puts down the book she was reading and answers the door. She opens the door and is surprised, "Hey, what brings you here this time of night and without calling?".

She says this jokingly, but she can see by the look on Carlos's face that he was in no mood to joke. She then realizes something is wrong, "What happened?".

"Can I come in?", Carlos says somberly. "Sure", Crystal steps backs and he walks into her apartment. He goes and sits down on the couch. Crystal sits beside him and caresses his face with her hand,

"Carlos…what happened?". "My father". Tears start streaming down his face, "My damn father".

"Sshh. It's okay. Don't say anymore", Crystal wraps her arms around Carlos. He continues to cry as if his father just died.

***

The sun is shining brightly as a new day begins. Carlos is asleep on the couch. Crystal emerges from her bedroom and checks on Carlos. She walks over to him and kneels down in front of the couch. She caresses his face with her lips and kisses him on the forehead.

He slowly opens his eyes and smiles. "Did you sleep well?", Crystal has a smile on her face. "I slept okay". "Do you want to tell me what happened?", Crystal says with concern. Carlos sits up. Crystal gets up and sits next to him.

***

Carlos sighs, "My father and I had an argument. You would think my father would put aside his pride and be happy for me. Happy that I've found someone who loves me. I respect my father's opinion, but not this time. If he wants to disown me, that's fine".

Crystal holds his hand, "Things will work out. For now, just close your eyes and take a deep breath". Carlos does what she says and then opens his eyes. "Feel better?". He looks at her, "A little".

Crystal takes a deep breath, "First of all…your father does not *own* you. You are a part of him genetically, but spiritually you are your own person. Secondly and forgive me for saying, but your father is a foolish and stubborn person. Your father is caught up in his own world like a lot of other people. I feel sorry for him, because he's going to miss out out on a lot".

Carlos nods his head, "That's true. He is". "Carlos, the only thing I can suggest is that you continue to love and respect…*yes*, respect your father", Crystal looks at him intensely. Carlos shakes his head in

47

disapproval, "I don't respect him anymore. I don't have respect for people like that".

***

"I know. But, he was responsible for bringing you into this world and raised you to be a strong, intelligent, caring, handsome man, who has good taste in women", Crystal grins at Carlos.

He smiles back, "You're so sweet. I just need time to think". "And that's a *good* thing. But in the meantime, I left a toothbrush, washcloth and towel on the bathroom sink. While you freshen up; I'll fix us something to eat". "Thank you, Crystal". "You're welcome", Crystal kisses Carlos on the forehead.

He gets up and goes into the bathroom. Crystal goes into the kitchen, gets juice out of the refrigerator and pours it into two glasses that she took out of the cabinet. She then takes out waffles and eggs, so she can cook them. While the waffles are in the waffle iron, she goes over to the radio that is in the living room and puts it on. She then goes back into the kitchen.

About 20 minutes later, Carlos comes out of the bathroom and Crystal has finished cooking breakfast. Carlos hears a beautiful love song on the radio and walks over to Crystal, "Come on. Come dance with me". "But the food is going to get cold", Crystal tells him, while putting the plates on the table. "It will only take a few minutes", Carlos takes her hand and pulls her out of the kitchen. "Cold eggs do not taste good".

"Then, I'll cook some more", Carlos embraces her and they start to dance. Crystal knows the song and sings it to Carlos. They are dancing cheek to cheek, while holding each other close.

Crystal then looks at Carlos, "I would have never known you had the hots for me, if we didn't get paired up".

Carlos chuckles, "Hots for you". "It's true. GOD don't makes mistakes. I will say one thing, I could not have gotten a better choice. I know there are going to be a lot more things to come, but at least we can share them together". Carlos gazes into Crystal's eyes, "I just realized something…I'm in love with you". "You're just now figuring that out. I could have told you that", Crystal has a smirk on her face. Crystal touches Carlos's face, "Oh and by the way…I'm in love with you, too".

Their faces slowly move closer together and they embrace into a deep kiss. What a way to forget one's troubles.

\*\*\*

At this point in time, Crystal and Carlos are inseparable. Carlos has found someone he can relate to and share his time with, so spending the day with Crystal was just where he wanted to be.

Time has passed quickly. Crystal and Carlos just finished eating dinner. "I'll clear the table", Carlos tells Crystal. "Well, thank you", Crystal says in a southern slang.

"You go sit down and relax", Carlos tells Crystal as he takes the dishes into the kitchen. Crystal goes and sits down on the couch. While Carlos is in the kitchen, Crystal puts on the radio. About 10 minutes later, Carlos comes out of the kitchen with a tray that has two plates of apple pie a la mode on it. He walks over to the coffee table and places down the tray.

"Mmmmm, yummy", Crystal sees the pie and licks her lips. "Dinner was delicious, baby", Carlos says lovingly. "I'm glad you enjoyed it. Are you ready for some pie?". "Absolutely",

Carlos sits down next to Crystal and she feeds him a piece of pie.

He raises his eyebrows as he takes the pie into his mouth and after he swallows the pie, he smiles. "Why are you smiling?", Crystal wipes his mouth with a napkin. "Because you're sweet just like this pie". Crystal bashfully lowers her head. There is a love song playing in the background and Carlos is thinking—**WHAT PERFECT TIMING**.

"I'd like to ask you something?". Crystal gives Carlos her undivided attention. "Really, what is it?". Carlos starts whistling and snapping his fingers.

\*\*\*

Crystal looks at him, "Are you alright?". Carlos then gets up, "Just listen to the song". Carlos starts singing and while Crystal is listening, Carlos bends down on one knee in front of Crystal. Crystal has figured out what he is about to do and starts to become teary-eyed.

"Crystal, GOD could not have sent me a *better* woman. You're intelligent, patient, loving, street savvy and most of all...beautiful. So, I'm asking...will you marry me?". Crystal grabs his face, "Yes. Yes, yes, yes, yes, si". Carlos jumps up and they kiss.

"I've got to call my mother and tell her the good news", Carlos says while holding Crystal. Crystal breaks away from Carlos, runs to get the phone tripping on her slippers along the way. She hands him the phone, "Are you going to be okay?". He looks at her, "I'm fine".

He dials the phone number and the phone rings three times, before it is answered. "Hello?". Carlos realizes that it is his mother and she was *just* the person he wanted to talk to.

He breathes a sigh of relief, "Hi, ma".

Carmen's face lights up, when she realizes who it is, "Hi, Carlito. How are you?. Are you okay?". "I'm fine, ma". His mother starts to sob, "I miss you being here in the house".

"I miss you too, ma. Ma, I have something to tell you. CrystaL and I are getting married".

His mother gets excited, "*Oh my GOD!*. Carlito, that's wonderful. You have my blessing. I love you, my son". "Thank you, mama. I love you, too. I'm going to be living with Crystal, so don't worry". "That's fine. As long as I know that you are safe. I hope to see you soon. I love you, Carlito", she starts to cry. "You will, ma. I'll talk to you soon", he hangs up the phone.

Carmen was in the livingroom, when she got the call from her son. As she hangs up the phone, her husband comes walking into the livingroom, "What's going on?. Why are you crying?". She wipes her face with her apron, "Well, I don't know if you care to know". He goes over and sits next to her, "Well, what is it?".

She clears her throat, " that was your son on the phone. He has informed me that he is getting married…to Crystal, so I gave him my blessing". If **looks could kill** as Carlos Sr. looks at his wife, "You're right. I *don't* care to know. You don't expect me to be happy, do you?".

"At this point, I don't expect anything from you. As long as my son is happy, I am happy". He *slaps* his knee, "Well, he is **not** getting my blessing". She gets up and stares down at him, "Why would he need your blessing. You **disowned** him, remember. You have a **lot** to learn. Good night". She walks away and goes upstairs. He yells out, ***"HE'S NO SON OF MINE!"***.

Well, the tides have turned and Carlos is the captain of his **own** ship. His father just had something **SPLASHED** in his face and it doesn't look like it had any positive affect on him. If Carlos Sr. is not careful, he could wind up being *shipwrecked* and that can be **VERY LONELY.**

*five*

Let the lovefest begin. Crystal and Carlos are **full steam ahead.** Nothing and no one can stop them from being with each other, except for **THAT** spirit which brought them together. Love is a beautiful thing, when it is unexpected and sincere.

Crystal knows that this is the man she wants to spend the rest of her life with and because she does not have the same issues in her family that Carlos has in his, it makes it all the more easier to love him. But for Carlos, he **will** defend his love for Crystal and that love will run **deeper** than any still water.

\*\*\*

It is a beautiful day to have a bridal shower and Crystal's family made sure that hers was a *blast*. The bridal shower is being held at her parent's home and the house is beautifully decorated. Crystal is amongst family, close friends and they have showered her with not just gifts, but a lot of love.

\*\*\*

The shower is about to end and Crystal's sister, Leslie who is petite and is known to the family as 'lil sis' stands up to give a speech.

"Alright, ladies. My sister, Crystal is at the end of her single life. So if there is anyone here who would like to wish her well, please take the floor. But before anyone does that, I'm going first. Crystal, you are a good woman. I had always hoped that one of us would get married and we're all glad it is you. Besides, I'm not ready to be locked down". The ladies start laughing.

Crystal turns up her nose, "Alright, alright". Her sister, Leslie finishes, "But seriously, you are getting a good man and I hope he takes good care of you. I love you very much and wish you all the peace, love and prosperity that GOD can bless you with". Leslie goes over to Crystal and hugs her. The ladies clap and the sound of **'AW'** fills the room.

One of Crystal's best friends, Vanessa quickly jumps up to speak before anyone else decides to, "Okay, it's my turn. Crystal, you're my homegirl and I love you dearly. But I have one question...you couldn't find any brothers?".

**OH BROTHER...*did somebody just throw a wrench?*.**

\*\*\*

All of a sudden, the room becomes quiet. Some of the ladies look at Crystal, some of the ladies look at Vanessa. **YOU COULD HEAR A PIN DROP**.

Crystal puts down a gift she had in her lap and looks straight at Vanessa, "Why are you going there?". Leslie interjects, "Must we have this discussion?. This is **not** the place nor the time". You can hear the other women start to mumble and talk amongst themselves. Vanessa quickly responds, "Yes, *we must*". Crystal slowly gets up, "No, *we will not*. Vanessa, this is not the time to be discussing your *own* personal issues".

Some of the women in the room say out loud, "Uh huh" and "That's right". Vanessa puts her hand on her hip, "Personal issues. I guess I have issues, because I love black men". "I love black men, too", Crystal says confidently. "You could have fooled me", Vanessa says sarcastically. "Vanessa has a point", Crystal's other friend, Denise puts her two cents in.

Crystal looks over at Denise, "Well, guess what. Both you and Vanessa can *point* yourselves in the direction of the door and escort yourselves out". Crystal points her finger towards the front door and some of the women chuckle and giggle.

Leslie steps in again, "Okay ladies, that's enough. Listen, my sister has the right to marry whomever she wants. As long as Carlos is good to her, that's all that matters". All of the women nod in agreement.

Crystal's mother comes out of the kitchen and sees that Crystal and Vanessa are standing, "How's things out here?". "Oh, just dandy mom". All of a sudden, everybody burst out into laughter and Crystal's mother doesn't have a clue as to what just happened. She looks around at everybody, "Are you all alright?". Leslie walks over to her mother, "Yes ma, everything is fine".

All of the ladies in the room are looking at Vanessa and at this point, Vanessa is starting to feel **MIGHTY small.** Vanessa takes a deep breath and exhales, "Crystal, I apologize for upsetting you. I did not mean it…especially not today. I'm sorry, girl". Vanessa starts getting teary-eyed. Crystal walks over to her and hugs her, "No hard feelings. I still love you". "I love you, too", Vanessa says while she wipes away her tears.

All of a sudden, there is an eruption of applause in the room. Crystal's mother looks at everyone, "Boy, this is some bridal shower. We need to have them more often". The ladies start to laugh.

Leslie wraps up the event, "That's so beautiful. Now, we are going to end the evening with a group dance". She goes over to the stereo and puts on a song. Everyone gets up and dances the electric slide.

Speaking of slide, it's not always easy to slide in and out of situations such as the one Crystal and Vanessa just had. It could have been worse. Thank goodness for the **LOVE** in the room. But, who's to say that it won't happen again.

*** 

At the other end of town, Carlos's buddies are throwing him a bachelor party. Carlos's friend, Ramone is the host of the event. It is being held at his house and there are about 40 '**estrogen**' hungry men in the house. Fortunately, the dancers have left and just for the record, they didn't dance *ON* Carlos. Carlos wasn't interested, so his buddies got all of the attention—**GOOD MAN**.

Ramone stands in front of the crowd to make a speech, "Alright, we are at the end…the end of the road for our brethren, Carlos. He has journeyed a long way to get to this point in his life. There's no turning back now for it is *too late*. Can I get an amen?". The guys in the room say, "Amen".

Carlos looks up at the ceiling and laughs, "Are you finished with my eulogy?". Ramone continues, "My brother, I'm just getting started. Now, is there anyone else here who would like to bid farewell to our brethren?".

One of Carlos's other friends, Chris raises his hand and walks up to the front of the room, "Yes. Carlos, we've been friends for a long, long time and I know it has not been easy for you to find yourself a good woman. But, I personally think you've found yourself a goldmine. I know Crystal and she's sweet, smart and sassy. I wish you both the best and may you have a lot of great times together. Here's to Carlos". He raises his glass. The rest of the guys raise their glasses and say, "To Carlos".

Carlos's cousin, Joseph gets up and starts preaching, "Carlos, Carlos, *oh Carlos*. You've gone and done it". He raises his hand in the air like he is about to get the 'Holy Ghost'. "I'm going to miss you, man", Joseph puts his hand over his face and starts shaking his head back and forth.

Some of the guys start laughing. Carlos is shaking his head and thinking—**YEP, HE'S RELATED TO ME**. Joseph takes his hand down from his face, "But in all seriousness, you couldn't find a Cuban woman?".

**HERE WE GO, AGAIN**

There is **dead silence** in the room. "Here we go, again", Carlos says outloud. "Joseph, what's your problem man?", Ramone comes to Carlos's defense. "I'm serious. Come on, Carlos. You're my cousin and I love you. I'm not saying Crystal is not a good person, but you know what *I mean?*".

Carlos *slowly* walks over to Joseph and stands right in front of his face, "No, **I don't know what you mean.** But I do know it's time for you to leave". He says this with such a thick Cuban accent that most of the guys that know Carlos know that **it is** time for Joseph to **BOUNCE** or he will get **bounced**.

Ramone steps in to resolve the situation, before it gets any worse, "No, nobody is leaving. Listen Joseph, we are not here to talk about other people's issues. Particularly, *YOUR* issues. We are here to have a good time. Nobody here is going to spoil my boy's night. There should be nothing but *love* in this room right now and if you don't have love…we'll give you some. Now, is there anybody else who needs to go on the Dr. Phil show to express their personal issues?".

Some of the guys chuckle. "Good, then it's agreed. This situation is closed". All the guys in the room say, "Agreed", except for Joseph. Joseph sighs and then looks at Carlos, "Agreed. Carlos I'm not trying to put a damper on your day". "You sure, cause it sounds like it's raining cats and dogs outside", Carlos says jokingly.

The guys burst out laughing. Joseph puts his arm around Carlos's shoulder, "Carlos…I love you dude". They hug each other. "Now, that's what I'm talking about", Ramone shouts out and then puts his arms around both Carlos and Joseph for a 'group' hug.

"There's nothing, but LOVE in this room", Ramone says with a smile and he starts to sing. Some of the guys are laughing, some are clapping, one is trying to put his hand over Ramone's mouth to keep him from singing.

Well, the evening was filled with love, laughter and **lecturing**. Lecturing on minding one's own business and letting others live their own lives. Crystal and Carlos have only just begun and they definitely are in good shape.

***

The weekend has past and it's Monday. Crystal and Carlos are getting ready to go out on patrol and as they are leaving the precinct, they are approached by another officer, "Crystal, Carlos. The Sarge wants to see the both of you right now!". Crystal and Carlos can see by the look on the officer's face that it must be important, so they don't hesitate to follow the officer back inside the precinct.

"Sure", Crystal says with concern. Carlos looks at Crystal, "I wonder what's up?". Crystal raised her eyebrows, "Who knows. This job is full of surprises".

They follow the officer to the conference room. The officer opens the door. Crystal and Carlos walk into a dark room. But all of a sudden; the lights go on and they hear, **"SURPRISE!"**. "*OH SHIT!*", Carlos blurts out. Crystal has her hands over her mouth as she sees the room full of her fellow officers.

The room is decorated with balloons, flowers, streamers and a sign that reads, '**CONGRATULATIONS**'. There is a long table stretched from one end to the other with lots of food on it. One of the female officers goes up to Crystal and pins a beautiful corsage on her shirt. One of the male officers pins a carnation flower on Carlos's shirt and shakes Carlos's hand.

There are two chairs that have been decorated with signs-one says 'BRIDE' and the other says 'GROOM'. Crystal sits down in 'her' chair and Carlos sits down in 'his' chair. There is

**THUNDEROUS** applause and cheering coming from their fellow officers and it becomes overwhelming for crystal for she starts to cry. Carlos is even becoming a little teary-eyed.

The Sarge is standing in front of the room, "Okay, everyone. Can I have your attention, please?". Everyone in the room quiets down. The Sarge sounds like a reverend presiding over a wedding, "We are gathered here today to congratulate two of our fellow officer, Crystal and Carlos on their engagement".

The Sarge is interrupted by applause from all of the officers in the room. The Sarge puts his hand up to quiet everyone, again. He resumes, "Nobody could not have picked two finer people to be with one another. I'm sure they will be dedicated to each other as they are to this job. Carlos, you better take care of my daughter. Don't let me have to come after you, because you don't want to feel the heat".

Everyone in the room starts laughing and saying, "Ooooooo". Even Crystal and Carlos are laughing. The Sarge tries to keep his composure, "Crystal is a good woman. It is not easy to find a pearl in the ocean, but you've found one. Treasure her and Crystal, you do the same. He comes from *MY* stock. Good stock".

The Sarge looks around the room, "Does everyone have a glass?". Everyone says, "Yes". "Good. Crystal and Carlos, please stand". Crystal and Carlos stand up and they hold each other's hand. The Sarge clears his throat, "All of us here wish you the best that life has to offer. That includes lots and lots of love. To Carlos and Crystal". All of the officers say, "To Carlos and Crystal" as they raise their glasses to toast the couple.

"Now, even though this is not the wedding, you must have one dance. Alright, cue the music", the Sarge makes a gesture with his hand and a song comes on. Everyone starts clapping and cheering as Carlos and Crystal walk to the middle of the room and start to slow dance.

There are flashes of light coming from the cameras that are being used to take pictures of Carlos and Crystal. Everyone soon quiets down. Crystal and Carlos are gazing into each other's eyes and their lips *lock* into a sweet kiss. The eruption of applause and cheers fills the room, again.

\*\*\*

While everyone is enjoying the festivities, an officer comes into the conference room with a piece of paper and he gives the paper to the Sarge. The Sarge reads it quietly and then asks the same officer to go and turn off the music.

The Sarge speaks in a stern, loud voice, "Excuse me, everyone. I hate to break up the festivities, but we have a serious situation taking place at a school. We have two to three gunmen holding about 50 children and two teachers as hostages. We are going to need a *FULL* team of officers out there. There will be officers that will stay behind to keep the precinct in operation. Carlos and Crystal; since you are already dressed for the environment, I'm putting you in there. Alright, ladies and gentlemen. Let's take this slow and easy. ***Let's move!***".

\*\*\*

The officers start leaving the room and the Sarge walks over Carlos and Crystal, "Listen, this is a dangerous situation you're going into. Take all of the necessary precautions you need to. Those gunmen at the school are heavily armed. I want those children and teachers out of there in one piece, not pieces. I'm sure you feel the same way. We'll have SWAT backing you up. Take care of each other and *be safe*".

The Sarge pats the both of them on the back. Carlos and Crystal leave the room. "Boy, some honeymoon", Carlos says with a smile. Crystal hits him on the back of the head. Crystal stops Carlos, "You know we're going to have to go in unarmed".

"Not exactly. Here, strap this piece to your ankle. The suspects won't be able to tell it's there", Carlos and Crystal a small gun. "What if we get searched?", Crystal says with concern. Carlos looks at her intensely, "Let's pray we don't". They hug each other and ***HOLD*** on for what seems like an eternity.

They kiss each other on the lips and head out the door. Danger is a *part* of the job and it is a job that both Carlos and Crystal are good at.

# *six*

████████████████████████████████

One of a police officer's worst fears is that someone has been taken hostage, especially if it's a child. So, there is no hesitation in responding to the crisis that was taking place at a public school. Carlos, Crystal, some of their fellow officers and SWAT are there in a matter of minutes. SWAT is being posted on the tops of roofs of buildings in the surrounding area of the school. Some of the officers from the precinct are being stationed in front and back of the school.

The Sarge is at ground level with Carlos and Crystal. There are cops cars everywhere and people from the neighborhood have crowded the sidewalks to watch the **drama** unfold. Parents of the students that are inside the school have already arrived to the school looking for their children. Some parents are crying, while others are in prayer in the hopes that the children will be released unharmed.

\*\*\*

The Sarge is surrounded by Carlos, Crystal, a Captain from SWAT and a few of the other officers. The Sarge wants to give a briefing, so that everyone is clear on *what* to do and what may be expected.

"Alright. The first thing that is going to be done before you go in is to establish communication with the gunmen. I will do that from out here.

If that proves to be successful, then I will send you in. Look to see exactly how many gunmen are inside and the condition of the children. I will give you a walkie-talkie to communicate with me. I am hoping that these guys are not trigger happy and just want their demands met. We already know *what* our agenda is, get those children and teachers out of there unharmed and apprehend the suspects. Let's hope that can be done without incident. Let's be prepared for the unexpected. Anything can *jump* off. Is everyone clear?".

Carlos, Crystal, the Captain and the other officers say, "Yes". The Sarge gets on the bullhorn, "Hello inside. This is Sergeant Murphy. We want to negotiate the release of the children and teachers. We want to send in two unarmed officers with a walkie-talkie. If you agree to this, please give us a sign".

When Crystal looks up, she sees a window opening up on the second floor, "Sarge, over there. Someone is coming to the window".

Crystal points to the window and all eyes are glued to **that** window to see what is going to happen next. One of the suspects sticks his head out of the window. He has a bandana tied around his face as to where you can only see his eyes, a gun in one hand and his other arm wrapped around a child. Unfortunately, the mother of that child is waiting outside the school. When she sees her child, she start to wail and scream out the child's name.

A police officer and other people try to comfort her. Crystal looks over at the mother, "We've got to get those children out of there".

The gunman speaks in a deep, loud voice, "I don't want any games played. If I see that's the case, these children won't see their next birthday. Send the officers in and **ONLY** them". Just as the gunman is about to go back inside, the child screams out, **"MOMMY!"**. The mother of that child cries even more. The gunman and the child disappears back into the school as the window closes.

The look on the Sarge's face is a look of relief, "Okay. That's what I wanted to see. The children are alive. Carlos, Crystal, move into position and watch each other's back. Everyone, take your positions".

Carlos and Crystal look at each other. Carlos winks at Crystal to reassure her that everything will be okay. Crystal smiles back. The Sarge hands Carlos a walkie-talkie. Crystal and Carlos head towards the school.

Crystal and Carlos are at the doors of the school. Carlos pulls on one of the doors and it opens, so they go inside. They walk up the stairs to the first floor to look around for anybody still left behind. They look in the guidance office to see if any staff are inside.

"Hello?", Crystal calls out, but no one responds. She goes inside and slowly looks around, but does not see anyone. "Hello, we are police officers. If there is anybody in here, please come out. We are not going to hurt you". She goes into the principal's office, but no one is there.

Carlos checks under one of the desks, when, "**AH!**". One of the school staff yells out, when she sees Carlos. Carlos raises his eyebrows, "Why didn't you answer the first time?". "I was afraid it was one of the gunmen trying to lure me out", she tells Carlos as he helps her out from underneath the desk.

"What is your position here at the school?". "I am one of the secretaries". Carlos looks her up and down to check to see if she had any bruises, "Are you alright?". "I'm fine. When the gunmen came into the school, they pointed their guns at the staff and told everyone to get out of the building. *I panicked.*

"I was afraid that one of them was going to shoot us in the backs, so I hid under my desk. They didn't bother to check the desks, because all of the staff ran out of the building. I was afraid to come out. I was able to reach on my desk and get my cell phone to call the police. Thank goodness I was able to do that".

Carlos smiles at her, "We are grateful that you did do that. Now, we can take care of this situation. Just relax a minute". Carlos sits the secretary down on a chair and then gets on the walkie-talkie, "Sarge, come in".

The Sarge responds, "Yes, Carlos?". "We found a school staff member unharmed. I'm sending her out. Pick up". "Good.Bring her to the door and we'll take it from there. Copy?".

"Copy", Carlos responds. The Sarge motions to the officers that are stationed at the front door that someone is coming out.

Carlos turns to the secretary, "Okay. I'm going to take you to the front door and the officers are going to take care of you. Are you ready?". "Yes. This has been quite an experience. I hope everything goes well. Good luck", the secretary gets up from the chair and goes with Carlos. "Yeah, thanks". Carlos takes her to the front door, knocks on the door three times and opens it. The lady goes to the awaiting officers. Carlos rejoins Crystal.

***

"I just remembered, the principal and vice principal are already outside", Carlos tells Crystal. Crystal and Carlos start walking down the hallway, going inside the classrooms, one by one. "We're all clear. Let's head upstairs", Crystal tells Carlos as he makes his way towards the stairs.

Upon entering the second floor; they move slowly, going inside each classroom and checking inside the closets. "So far, so good. Most of children were released along with the staff", Carlos tells Crystal. They go into the gym; look under the bleachers, check the locker rooms, but it is completely empty. "Nobody in here. Let's continue looking in the rest of the classrooms", Crystal makes her way out of the gym with Carlos following close behind.

As they head down the hall checking the rest of the classrooms, Crystal stops in front of one of the classroom door's and then ducks back. She signals Carlos to come over to her. She whispers to him, "This classroom is filled with children. They are sitting on the floor. I saw three teachers standing in the back of the classroom. I also saw one gunman, who was holding a semi-automatic".

"I wonder how many more gunmen are in there", Carlos looks towards the door. "I'm going to have another look", Crystal moves slowly back towards the door. She stands to the side of the door and looks through the glass window.

Some of the children see her and start to look excited, but Crystal puts her finger on her lips as a sign to the children to stay quiet. She nods to them and smiles. Carlos and Crystal look at each other. "Are you ready?", Carlos holds up his hand. "As ready as I'll ever be", Crystal locks hands with him.

Carlos knocks on the door and one of the gunmen walks over to the door and looks to see who it is. He sees Carlos and Crystal and walks away from the door. The door slowly opens and the gunman waves to them to come in.

The look on the children's faces say everything for they can see that Crystal and Carlos are the '**good guys**'. Carlos and Crystal walk in and notice that there are two gunmen in the room. "Welcome", one of the gunmen says to them. Crystal also notices some of the children are crying, while others are smiling. All of the children are sitting on the floor. The other gunman's face is covered with a bandana and he has on dark glasses.

Having the spirit of a concerned mother, Crystal asks the children if they are alright. Some of the children nod their heads, some respond, "Yes". One of the children talks to her,

"Are you going to take us home?". Crystal bends down to where the child is sitting, "Don't worry, you're going to go home soon".

***

Carlos scans the room with his eyes and counts around 50 children. Carlos turns to one of the gunmen, "Alright, we are here to listen to your demands. We want to get these children back home to their parents, so I hope this can go sweet and simple".

The gunman responds, "That's good. I have no intentions on harming these children as long as everybody plays along nicely. As you can see, *I* don't have on any glasses. I'm not afraid to look at a piece of shit". The gunman has a grimacing smile on his face, "First, we want a car filled with a full tank of gas to get *US* to the airport. No plates on the car. US meaning my partner and I, two children and *this* beautiful lady".

The gunman points to Crystal. Carlos objects quickly, "She's not a part of the negotiation". The gunman moves closer to Carlos's face with a gun in his hand, "She is now. Is there a problem?". Carlos looks over at Crystal with **GREAT** concern as she looks at him. He then looks back at the gunman, "No problem".

The gunman continues with his demands, "I want a private jet and the pilot better *NOT* be an undercover cop. In the plane, I want three million dollars in small bills, unmarked of course". Carlos is disgusted, but he tries not to show it on his face, "Is that all?".

***

"I think that should be sufficient. I will tell the pilot where we are headed. Once we are safely on the plane, I will let the children and your partner go. You see, I'm not so bad". The gunman takes a step back from Carlos.

"Question, why does she have to go?", Carlos says to the gunman in a calm voice as he points to Crystal. "Because she is our insurance and bodyguard. Uhm". Carlos **looks** at the gunman as if he wants to finish him off right then and there.

Crystal looks at the gunman, "It's cool. Now if I go with you, will let these children and teachers go?". "Sure. You wash my hands, I'll wash your body", the gunman says sarcastically as he looks at Crystal up and down.

Carlos is **SEETHING** and he is saying to himself—**I'M READY TO PUT THIS GUY'S LIGHTS OUT!.** The children start to look excited. "Is it okay if I talk to my Sergeant?", Crystal holds up the walkie-talkie. "Sure. Just keep it clean", the gunman says in a stern voice.

Crystal talks into the walkie-talkie, "Sarge. This is Crystal, copy". The Sarge responds, "I hear you Crystal, go ahead". "The gunmen are willing to let the children and teachers go, with the exception of two children and me. They want to use us as insurance".

The Sarge pauses for a moment for he does **NOT** like the sound of that. The other officers standing around him hear this and have a look of concern. "Sarge?", Crystal is wondering why the Sarge has not responded. The Sarge clears his throat, "I heard you Crystal. Are you going to be okay?".

Carlos is *looking* at Crystal the whole time, while she is talking to the Sarge and Crystal responds back with a smile, "I'm going to be fine. The gunmen want a car filled with a full tank of gas to get to the airport. They want a jet ready to go with a *clean* pilot. We were told that we will be let go, once they are safely on the jet".

"Let us know when they are ready to send the children and teachers out", the Sarge is biting his lip. "I will-" Crystal is about to get off the walkie-talkie, when the gunman that was talking to her puts his hand out towards Crystal, "I want to talk to him". Crystal hands the walkie-talkie to the gunman, "Uh Sarge, this is one of the gunman. How are you?".

The Sarge is thinking—**OH, HE REALLY IS A WISE ASS.** The Sarge responds, "I should be asking you that". "Don't worry, Sarge. I'm taking good care of her. *GOOD* care of her", he turns off the walkie-talkie and gives it back to Crystal. The gunman smirks at Carlos.

\*\*\*

The gunman looks around at everyone and raises his voice, "Okay, this is the deal. 12 children can go at a time with you". He points to Carlos. "With the exception of two children. *These* two children", the gunman points to two children that are sitting in the back.

They start to cry. The other gunman with the dark glasses on *mocks* the children, "Please, don't cry. I can't stand it, when children cry. They sound like whimpering bitches". Both Carlos and Crystal raise their eyebrows as high as they could go. Carlos makes a fist with his hand. Crystal looks at him and *slowly* shakes her head, 'No'.

The other gunman speaks, "Once the children are all out, then the teachers can leave. Fair enough?". Crystal responds, "Fair". The other gunman speaks, "I don't want any funny business and don't do anything stupid. Because I know how to get *STUPID*". The gunman cocks his gun and the children gasps. Carlos is saying to himself—**YEAH, YOU'RE STUPID ALRIGHT.**

Carlos asks for the walkie-talkie from Crystal and she hands it to him. "Sarge, this is Carlos. Come in". The Sarge picks up, "Go ahead, Carlos". "I'm coming down with 12 children at a time, so get ready. Copy". "We'll be on stand by. That's a copy".

\*\*\*

The Sarge gets on the bullhorn, "Okay everyone, listen up. Those of you at the door, get ready. Carlos is coming out with 12 children. He will be bringing out 12 children at a time. Let's be on point". The officers are in their positions. SWAT continues to keep a close eye from various roofs around the neighborhood. The Sarge closes his eyes in hopes of an *easy* resolution to this crisis.

Back in the classroom, Crystal walks to the front of the classroom, so that she can have the children's attention. She talks in a cheerful voice, "Hi everybody. My name is Crystal and I know a lot of you are scared. But, I have good news. Most of you are going home". Most of the children start clapping and their faces brighten up. "With the exception of the two children in the back, who are being taken by the gunmen." They start to cry and a teacher consoles them.

Crystal quiets them down, "Okay everyone, relax. Now, what I'm going to do is start counting and I'm going to stop at the number 12. When I come around and touch your head, you stand up. Okay?". The children say, "Okay". Crystal starts walking from one end to the other tapping the children on their heads, "1,2,3,4,5,6,7,8,9,10,11,12". Those children stood up.

Crystal points to Carlos, "Now, you see that nice fellow over there. He is going to escort you into the hallway, downstairs and then outside. So those of you who are standing, make a line in front of him". The children line up in front of Carlos. The gunmen are watching Crystal and Carlos's

68

*every* move. The teachers look happy to see the children that the children are leaving.

Carlos smiles at the children, "Hi everyone. I'm that nice fellow. I know all of you are excited, but I don't want you to push the person in front of you. Just follow me and walk slowly". Carlos walks towards the door, opens it and the children follow him into the hallway. One of the gunman follows closely behind the children and stands in the hallway.

Carlos walks back over to the glass window. Crystal is standing in front of the window and they look at each other eye to eye. He blows her a kiss and *then all of a sudden*, Crystal is **pushed** aside and he sees the other gunman looking at him eye to eye. He has a *creepy* smirk on his face. Carlos turns away from him and puts his attention back to the children.

Carlos talks to the children, "Now, when I give you the signal, you are going to jog down the stairs, not run. I don't want any of you to get hurt. You are going to jog right out the front door. There will be police officers waiting for you to take you to your parents. Okay?".

Some children nod, while other say, "Okay". Carlos gets on the walkie-talkie, "Sarge, I'm coming down with the first set of children". "Copy". The Sarge gets on the bullhorn, "Okay, the children are coming down!".

Back inside the school, the children look anxious to get out of the school. Carlos takes a deep breath, "Okay kids. On the count of three, 1..2..3. Let's go!". The children follow Carlos down the stairs and to the first floor. Carlos knocks on the front door three times and pushes the front door open. The children start **running** out the door like doves being released from a cage.

They run into the awaiting arms of officers, who are posted by the door. The officers escort them to the police vans that are parked across the street from the school. Some of the children start crying hysterically, while others smile happily. Carlos sees the Sarge, give him a '**thumbs up**' and goes back inside the school.

Carlos heads back upstairs and just as he gets to the second floor stairwell, he hears the Sarge on the walkie-talkie. "Carlos, come in". Carlos answers, "Yes Sarge, copy". "Listen, I know why the gunmen want to take Crystal. It makes for an *easy* exit for them, but a *hard* risk for us".

Carlos pauses and then responds, "They are using her as bait. I'm **NOT** going to let that happen". The Sarge reassures Carlos, "Don't worry, Carlos. We're **NOT** going to let anything happen to her. We are going to get her back safe and sound. You and I know that". "I know *WE* will, Sarge". "Keep me posted. Copy", the Sarge tunes out.

Carlos walks back to the classroom and notices nothing strange. "Okay, I'm ready for the next set". Crystal counts out 12 more children, they follow Carlos into the hallway, down the stairs to the front door and outside to the awaiting officers. Carlos continues this pattern and while he is downstairs, Crystal talks to the 'head' gunman.

"Can I ask you a question?. Why do you want to take these two children?", Crystal motions her head to the two children in the back of the classroom. The gunman looks at the children and then at Crystal, "I specifically picked them, because this one has a smart mouth and this one kept giving me dirty looks. I thought I'd teach them a lesson for today. The gunman looks back at the children and smiles.

Crystal walks over to the children and puts her arms around them. Both children **hold** Crystal tightly like a bear hug. Carlos arrives back upstairs and takes the last set of children downstairs. He heads back upstairs to get the teachers.

As Carlos is escorting the teachers downstairs, one of the teachers speaks to him, "Is she going to be alright?". Carlos looks at her with confidence, "She is going to be fine". Carlos escorts the teachers outside and heads back upstairs.

He goes back into the classroom. The 'head' gunman speaks like a sly fox, "well, that went rather smoothly. Let's keep up the good work. I'm ready, when you are". Carlos gets on the walkie-talkie, "Sarge, is the car ready?". The Sarge responds quickly, "It's ready. They can come out". Carlos answers, "Copy".

Carlos looks at the both gunmen, "Alright, guys. Your car is ready". "Wonderful. Alright everyone, it's time for us to go on our field trip", the gunman with the dark glasses opens the door. Carlos walks through first followed by the two children, Crystal and the other gunman.

The gunmen did not see, but Crystal managed to *grab* one of the erasers from the chalk board ledge and tuck it inside her pants. Everyone is walking towards the stairs, when all of a sudden Crystal is stopped by the 'head' gunman. The gunman calls over to his partner, "You take the officer and the children to the stairwell. I want to talk to Crystal alone".

Carlos steps up to the 'head' gunman, "I *don't* think that's necessary". The gunman **cocks** his gun and says this in a deep voice, "Oh, but **IT** is!. The gun is pressed against Carlos's chin. Crystal steps in, "Carlos, it's okay. You go with the children. I'll be fine". Carlos looks at Crystal *intensely* and backs away slowly. The other gunman grabs Carlos by the arm and takes him back to the stairwell.

The gunman backs Crystal up against a wall. Crystal is looking at the gunman eye to eye, "What do you want to talk about?". The gunman is holding his gun with one hand and has the other hand on Crystal's chin, "Who said anything about talking?. I'm sure you know how men can get sometimes, especially when it comes to seeing a beautiful woman such as yourself. Men get urges sometimes".

Crystal responds carefully, "I'm sure they do, but what does that have to do with me?". He moves closer to her face, "It has a *lot* to do with you. I need something right now that I'm sure you will be able to give me". Crystal tilts her head, "I'm sorry, but I probably wouldn't be of any help to you. I'm a lesbian". The gunman looks at her funny, "Oh, you got jokes.

You smell really nice". The gunman is **sniffing** Crystal like a dog in heat.

***

From a distance, the other gunman is looking through the glass window of the door watching what is going on between his partner and Crystal, "I wish I could have a taste of that".

He has his back turned to Carlos and the two kids. Carlos motions to the two kids to stay quiet and he moves closer to the gunman. The gunman has no idea what Carlos is doing for he is too busy being nosy.

His partner is still hitting on Crystal, "Now, all you have to do is keep still and I'll take care of the rest". "The rest of what?", Crystal says sarcastically. The gunman zips down the front of his pants and Crystal is thinking—**YOU STUPID, HORNY TOAD.**

Crystal takes out the eraser that she has hidden in the back in her pants and **hits** him a couple of times in the face blinding him. The gunman **jumps** back rubbing his eyes, *"OH SHIT, MY EYES"*. Crystal aims straight for his groin with a front snap kick and then grabs the gun out of the gunman's hand. The gunman drops to his knees **groaning** in pain, "**OH**, my nuts!. You stupid bitch".

Crystal kneels down to the suspect's face, "If I were you, I wouldn't call anybody else stupid, stupid. It's over". The suspect tries to grab Crystal's arm, but she *knocks* his hand away, pushes him on his stomach and handcuffs him.

The other gunman is still looking from the stairwell, "Oh shit, she just wrestled down my boy. Oh hell no!". The gunman is about to open the door, when he feels someone tap him on the shoulder. When he turns around, it is Carlos, "Can I have a look?". Carlos then **punches** him in the face *twice* and grabs the gun out of his hand. The suspect is dazed.

He holds the gun to the suspect's face, "You should have been paying better attention. **ON THE FLOOR, NOW!**". The suspect drops to the floor, Carlos takes out a pair of 'plastic' handcuffs and handcuffs him. The two children start cheering, "Yeah!". Carlos picks the suspect up from the ground, "If I were you, I would not get any bright ideas, so stay quiet. Oh, I'm sorry. You wouldn't know anything about being *bright*". The suspect gives him a nasty look.

Carlos gets on the walkie-talkie, "Sarge, we got both suspects down.

I'm sending the two children downstairs, first. Then, Crystal and I will be out with the suspects". *"GREAT JOB, Carlos!"*. Carlos puts the suspect back on his stomach and turns to the children, "You kids head downstairs. There are police officers waiting outside to help you. *Go!*". The kids run downstairs as fast as their legs could carry them.

Carlos goes through the door to see how Crystal is doing, "Not bad for a city gal". "Oh, you're funny. Where are the kids and the suspect?", Crystal looks around Carlos's shoulder.

"The kids are outside safe and the suspect is right behind that door on the floor", Carlos nods his head. "Good work, my man. You should not have left your suspect". "Oh, don't worry. I have his ankles tied around the stairwell pole. The Sarge is waiting for us to bring these suspects downstairs". "Well, let's get moving", Crystal picks up her suspect off the ground.

They walk through the door, Carlos retrieves his suspect and they head downstairs. They take the suspects outside to their fellow officers, who take the suspects into custody. When the crowd sees Carlos and Crystal comes out with the suspects, they cheer loudly.

Carlos and Crystal walk over to the Sarge. "Sarge, we have to head back upstairs. There is still one more floor to check", Crystal says quickly. "The both of you *be careful*. You did great. I'll see you in a few", the Sarge gives them a 'thumbs up'.

Carlos and Crystal head back inside the school. They go upstairs to the third floor, which is the last floor that has classrooms. They start walking around, checking the classrooms one by one to see if anyone else was left behind.

**There is a figure standing in a corner between two small walls...**

Carlos is at the end of the hall and Crystal has walked down to the other end of the hall to cover ground quicker. Their backs are turned, when the **'figure'** comes out of the corner. Crystal turns around and sees the person. He is raising something and Crystal sees that it is a...gun.

He is **pointing** the gun at Carlos and Crystal screams to the top of her lungs, **"CARLOS DUCK, HE HAS A GUN!"**. Just as Carlos turns around, the gun has already fired and the bullet **SLAMS** into Carlos's chest so hard that it sends him flying into midair backwards a few feet, before he falls to the ground. The sound of him hitting on the ground vibrates off the walls-

**BOOM!**

Crystal pulls out the gun from her ankle and **SHOOTS** the suspect in both thighs and he falls face forward to the ground. The gun flies out his hand and Crystal **runs** as fast as she can to retrieve the gun.

The suspect is moaning in pain. Crystal walks over to the suspect, "**DAMN**, there were three!". She grabs the suspect's wrists, put them behind his back and handcuffs him.

***

She looks over at Carlos and **runs** over to him. She sees that he is still. She kneels down near his mouth and hears him breathing **heavily.** She picks up the walkie-talkie that is beside him, **"CARLOS IS DOWN, CARLOS IS DOWN!. NEED ASSISTANCE**-(she starts getting emotional) **NEED AN AMBULANCE, NOW!"**.

She drops the walkie-talkie, sits down on the ground and puts Carlos's head on her lap. Even though he had on a bullet—proof vest, blood is **streaming** out through his vest from the middle of his chest. Crystal has a handkerchief in her pocket, she takes it out and puts it over the wound. She wipes the sweat from his head forehead with her other hand, "Hey…you're going to be fine".

The tears start streaming down her face and onto Carlos's face like raindrops on a pond. She wipes the tears drops from his face and tries to fight back the tears. He **slowly** opens his eyes, but blood is coming out of the side of his mouth. He whispers, "Yeah…I know. Listen…you know…I love you". "Of course, I know. Sshh, don't talk. Try to reserve your energy. You're going to need it for our honeymoon", Crystal chuckles. Carlos tries to laugh, but starts to cough and spits up blood. She wipes the blood from his mouth.

\*\*\*

Crystal looks around, "**Damn**, where is the ambulance?. It seems like forever". Crystal can hear sirens outside and then she hears footsteps coming towards her and Carlos. She turns her head and sees her fellow comrades running down the hall.

She looks back at Carlos, "They're here. You hear me. You're going to be alright". *All of a sudden*, she feels someone touch her shoulder and when she looks up…it's the Sarge. "You come with me", he says in a soft voice. "I can't leave him", Crystal says somberly.

She sees two EMS medics running down the hall with a stretcher. It seems like they are moving in *slow* motion. They arrive to Carlos. She gets up and moves away, so the EMS can get to him. She knows there is nothing she can do, but **PRAY**.

"You…come…with…me. He's going to be fine. Come on", the Sarge puts his arm around Crystal's waist and the other hand he uses to hold her hand. They *slowly* walk away from Carlos. She looks over her shoulder and sees EMS staff working on him. She mouths to Carlos, "I love you, baby".

Crystal is saying to herself—**GOD WOULDN'T GIVEN ME MY SOULMATE JUST TO TAKE HIM AWAY.** She shall soon see…

# *seven*

███████████████████████████████████████████

...a day, a cloudy day. The sun is trying to peek through the clouds, but the clouds are *very* demanding. There is a calm breeze outside as the limousines pull up to the church. People are coming from all over, the city and country to take part in this emotional event. People, strangers and kin alike hug each as they enter the church. Police motor cycles and cars line both sides of the street to give respect to one of their own.

One of the limos has been set aside and is draped with flowers for that person who is being honored. As the people make their way into the large church, they are greeted by ushers who kindly show them to their seats. There is a long runner rug that stretches from the back of the church, which is the entrance all the way to the front of the church, where the pastor is standing.

The church is **FULL** to capacity and it is so full that there are people standing in the back of the church. There are a few police officers lined up along the walls on both sides of the church. It is quite a sight to see. Standing near the pastor to his left are eight nicely dressed men in their suits and to his right are eight beautifully dressed women in their dresses.

A man approaches the pastor and the pastor kindly asks, "Are you ready?". The man replies, "Absolutely". The pastor asks everyone in the church to stand up and there is a woman with a microphone who begins to sing.

What a **WONDERFUL** and joyous day to have a…WEDDING. That man who is standing next to the pastor and is glowing like a knight in shining armour is…CARLOS. He smiles to two people, who are seated directly across from him…his mother…*and* father.

Carmen wipes the tears from her eyes for she is a proud mother to have her son not just get married, but to have **ALIVE.** Miracles have definitely played a part in the lives of Carlos and Crystal. It is a miracle that Carlos survived his *demise* (he was pronounced dead at the hospital, but was brought back to life) and it was a miracle to see his father at the wedding. Carlos Sr. smiles at his son knowing that he **LOVES** his son *more* than he loves himself.

Everyone close to Crystal and Carlos is in attendance at this wedding, even the Mayor. When he heard about Carlos taking a bullet and almost dying while on duty, he felt compelled to show his gratitude. There are so many people that Carlos and Crystal may have needed a stadium for this event. The best man; Carlos's buddy, Ramone is there by his side and the maid of honor; Crystal's friend, Vanessa is there for her girl.

Everyone's attention is drawn to the beautiful flower girl walking down the aisle, who is Crystal's niece and right behind her is the ring bearer, who is Carlos's nephew. It was suggested that they be the last people to come out before the **star** attraction.

Here she comes…being accompanied by her father. She is draped in a beautiful gown that is embroidered in gold, especially designed for a *QUEEN*. She is **BEAMING** as she approaches her soulmate, the man she hopes to spend the rest of her life with. And yes…she is shining just like her name, CRYSTAL.

As she stops right in front of the pastor, her father kisses her on both sides of her face and then sits down in the front row next to her mother.

She takes her place across from her soon-to-be husband. The woman who was singing has become silent and the pastor tells everyone to be seated.

Carlos says to Crystal in a low voice, "You look absolutely beautiful". Crystal responds, "You do, too" and she blows him a kiss. The pastor begins, "Well, is this a beautiful day or what?". Everyone in the church responds loudly, "Yes". He continues on, "Today is a very, very special day. Not only do we have a blessing today, but a miracle, too". Some people in the church say, "Amen".

He goes on, "Now, I know you don't want to hear a sermon before a wedding, but you're going to hear one today. It's going to be brief, but believable. It's a blessing to see these two people here before us today. Why, because only *ONE* of them should be here and if that was the case, there would be no wedding. So, that's why it is a **MIRACLE** that Carlos stands here today before his wife, Crystal. For this I can say…we are gathered here today to witness the coming together of a man and a woman. Both whom GOD has decided belong together. Before I go any further, the couple has something they wanted to express to each other. Carlos".

Carlos is looking straight into Crystal's eyes and he clears his throat, "To my darling wife, Crystal.
I woke up one morning
as the rays of the sun came down
and so did an angel
and that angel was you
may my angel continue to comfort me
be still with me
and love me as I love you
GOD could not have sent me a more beautiful angel
may we be together, always".

After Carlos finishes; Crystal speaks, "To my beautiful husband,
There was you
all the time
in my view

your love was right on time
you've filled my life with so much joy
you are my man and my lover
I pray that there will be no other
man for me
you see
I am
You are
It is just…us".

"Boy, I don't know about you. But as far as I'm concerned, they're already married", the pastor says confidently. There is praise coming from the people in the church and some nod their heads in agreement. Tears are streaming down Crystal's face and Carlos wipes them away with his hand. Carlos has tears streaming down his face and Crystal wipes them away with her hand. You can hear people in the church sniffling and there is not a dried eye in the place.

The pastor continues, "Carlos, do you take Crystal as your wife. To honor her, respect her, in sickness and in health, for richer or poorer, til death due you part as long as you both shall live?". Carlos takes Crystal's hand, "I most certainly will" and he puts a ring on Crystal's finger.

The pastor smiles, "Crystal, do you take Carlos as your husband. To honor him, respect him, in sickness and in health, for richer or poorer, til death due you part as long as you both shall live?". "I most certainly will", Crystal places a ring on Carlos's finger.

Some of the people in the church give a '***halleujah***' shout. The pastor closes out the ceremony, "In the spirit of the Almighty Creator, I now pronounce you man and wife". Carlos and Crystal slowly embrace into a kiss and everyone is the church cheers and claps. The sound is so **THUNDEROUS** that the pastor covers his ears. After a few minutes of applause, the pastor holds up his hands and everyone quiets down. The pastor says, "I present to you, Mr. and Mrs. Ruiz".

There is an ***eruption*** of applause again as Carlos and Crystal get in a few more kisses. They turn and face everyone in the church. Right in front of their feet is a broom and they jump over it honoring an African custom. They start walking down the aisle and the people at the end of each row shake Carlos's hand and hug Crystal as they walk by.

\*\*\*

Their parents and the bridal party follow behind them as they exit the church. All of the guests slowly make their way out of the church and the sun decides to break through the clouds boldy. The sun has told the clouds goodbye and is **beaming** on the beautiful couple to make it a more beautiful day.

Because Crystal is a nature lover, instead of rice being (rice chokes birds), people are throwing flower pedals at the happy couple. Pictures are being taken as they get into their limousine…which is the one draped with flowers and has the sign, 'JUST MARRIED' on the back of it.

Their parents and the bridal party get into the other limos and they take off. Family and friends wave at them and will soon join them at the reception hall.

# *eight*

---

**IT IS TIME TO P.A.R.T.Y!.** Family, friends and neighbors have packed the reception hall to capacity and for 400 people, that is a lot of people who will be getting their *groove* on. There is a DJ playing music from the 60's, 70's, 80's and 90's. People are mingling, taking pictures and video taping.

The colors for the wedding are baby blue, lavender and gold. The table for the bridal party is absolutely beautiful. There is a candle with the date of the wedding, Carlos and Crystal's name on it to celebrate their union.

A few minutes later, the music stops and Ramone, Carlos's best friend is the host for the reception. He makes an announcement, "Please everyone. Those of you who are standing, can you take your seats. The bride and groom have arrived. Let me introduce myself, I am Carlos's right hand man, Ramone (*he says this humorously in a thick Cuban accent*). I personally want to thank all of you for coming to celebrate our brother and sister, Carlos and Crystal. Oh and on your way out, you can leave my tip at the door. Thank you".

Everyone erupts into laughter. Ramone gets a signal that the bridal party is ready to enter the hall. Ramone raises his hand for everyone to quiet down. *All of a sudden,* eight officers come marching into the hall and stand in formation of four officers on each side to form an aisle. They hold up their batons like a tunnel to a bridge, so that the bridal party can walk through…**SO COOL!**.

Ramone continues, "Ladies and gentlemen, I would like to present to you the parents of Mrs. Ruiz, that's Crystal if you didn't know". People start laughing and clapping at the same time as Crystal's parents walk through the formation. "Next; we have the parents of the groom, Mr. and Mrs. Ruiz". They walk through the formation and surprisingly, Carlos Sr. is *glowing* like a proud papa.

"Next, we have the maid of honor and since I can't be in two places at one time, Vanessa you hold it down". Vanessa smiles at Ramone as she walks through the formation. "Next, we have the bride's maids and ushers". They walk through the 'tunnel' in pairs and they take their seats at the bridal table.

"Ladies and gentlemen. Last, but not least we have Ken and Barbie", Ramone says jokingly. Everyone in the hall bursts out into laughter. "Oooops, just kidding. I am very happy to present to you, Mr. and Mrs. Ruiz". Everyone is standing on their feet applauding as Carlos and Crystal walk through the 'tunnel'.

Ramone is smiling at the couple as they reach the end of the formation. Carlos hugs Ramone and Ramone kisses Crystal on the cheek. Carlos and Crystal sit right in the middle of the bridal table. The 'tunnel' of officers break their formation and exit the hall. What a sight to see!.

Ramone gets back on the microphone, "Is everyone having a good time?". Everyone in the hall cheers and claps loudly. "Now, that's what I want to hear. Everyone can be seated".

Everyone on the hall sits down, except for the police officers. They come back into the hall and are standing near the entrance of the hall.

Ramone continues, "We are going to do things a little differently. We are going to start off with best wishes to the couple. I'm going first. Are there any objections?. Oh okay, I thought not". A few people chuckle.

Ramone turns to Carlos and Crystal, "Carlos, you're my homey, my buddy, my right hand man, man".

Carlos is thinking—**OH BOY, LET ME PUT ON MY SEATBELT.** Ramone clears his throat, "I've seen all of the women you've dated…and it has not been many. But, you definitely got yourself a queen. Treat her as well as you treat your mother. I since I know how you treat your mother; Crystal, you are in *good* hands. She has already given you so much happiness and I'm sure there's a lot more where that came from".

\*\*\*

Ramone raises his wine glass, "To Carlos and Crystal. Many years and many children. Cheers". Everyone in the hall says, "Cheers". "Okay, who is going to be next, because I'm a tough act to follow", Ramone smirks. People start laughing, again.

Carlos's father quickly stands up and the room becomes so quiet that you can hear a pin drop. Carlos Sr. walks over to Ramone and Ramone hands him the microphone. Carlos Sr. clears his throat, "My son-". He starts to get choked up and his eyes fill up with tears.

He keeps his composure, "I know that I have not been your biggest fan, especially in the past two years. I have not been very supportive, when it came to you and Crystal. A father always wants what is best for his child and I've realized that…you did get *the best*. Crystal, you have made my son very happy and that's what makes me happy. I love you my son and I love you too, Crystal. But most of all…I hope you can forgive me".

Carlos slowly gets up and walks over to his father. His father is crying and Carlos embraces him, "I forgive you, pop. I love you". There is a *thunderous* applause as people begin to stand up. Some people are crying. Carmen wipes the tears from her eyes. Crystal gets up, walks over to where her husband and father-in-law are. After Carlos releases his father, she then hugs him and Carlos Sr. hugs her back.

\*\*\*

**WHAT A MOMENT IN TIME.** After their embrace, Carlos's father goes and sits back next to his wife. Carlos and Crystal go and sit back in their seats. Ramone has a napkin in one hand wiping the tears from his eyes and a microphone in the other, "That was beautiful man".

\*\*\*

Everyone has long finished eating and is dancing the night away. Crystal's friend, Raymond whom she befriended arrives to the reception hall late. Crystal sees him from a distance, waves at him and he waves back. Carlos's father sees Raymond and has a strange look on his face. He is staring at Raymond as if he knows him and the *look* on his face turns into **ANGER.**

Carlos's father is dancing with his wife, but breaks away from her. He *rushes* over to Raymond and screams at him, **"WHAT IN THE HELL ARE YOU DOING HERE?!"**. Raymond looks at him, "I was invited-". Before Raymond could get out the next word, without warning Carlos's father **PUNCHES** Raymond in the face and Raymond goes down.

Carlos's father hits him again and Raymond blurts out, "What are you doing?!". The DJ sees what is going on and stops the music. People stop dancing, once the music stops and look around to see why the music stopped so abruptly. They see what is happening. Carlos and Crystal look at each other strangely, once they realize the music has stopped.

Carlos and Crystal turn around to see people gathering around in a circle and some of the people are saying, **"Stop!, stop!"**. Carlos realizes something is wrong and rushes over to see two people holding his father. **"YOU SON OF A BITCH. YOU'VE GOT SOME NERVE SHOWING UP HERE. WHAT ARE YOU DOING HERE?!"**, Carlos's father *screams* out.

Ramone and another person help Raymond up from the floor and Crystal has joined her husband's side. Carlos looks at his father, "*Pop, what are you doing?!*". "What do you mean what am I doing?. Why is this **bastard** here?!. **HE RAPED YOUR MOTHER!**", Carlos Sr. yells at his son.

From the waiters to the waitresses to all of the other people at the hall, everyone has a **SHOCKED** look on their faces. Carlos's face turns into *anger, "He what?!".* Without notice,

Carlos **PUNCHES** Raymond in the face before Raymond could say anything. "Carlos, *don't*. What is going on here?", Crystal grabs Carlos's arm just as he is about to hit Raymond, again.

By this time, Carmen has come to her husband's side, "Carlos, no. **NO!**. He didn't…he didn't do it". Carlos Sr. looks at his wife in disbelief, "What do you mean he didn't do it?".

Carlos looks at his mother and father with a *puzzled* look on his face, **"WHAT IS GOING ON HERE?!".** Carmen puts her hand on her husband's face and talks softly, "He didn't do it. I did not know how to tell you. That day at the precinct, when they had the line up…I just picked him out.

Because of you…**YOU**. It's you. This hate. The hate you've had for so long". Some people start shaking their heads. Carlos Sr. realizes what he has done to her, "But Carmen, why did you wait so long to tell me?. Oh my GOD. Look what I've done. I'm sorry, Carmen. I…am…so…sorry".

They embrace one another and he cries. Carlos and Crystal look at each other in shock. Some people start crying, some people start hugging each other. Raymond is sitting down in a chair, holding an ice pack to his face, when Carlos walks over to him, "Raymond, I don't know what to say. There's been a *BIG* mistake. I am sorry, man".

Raymond extends his hand, "It's cool. Just don't hit me, again". Carlos bends down and gives him a hug. Carmen is wiping her husband's face and she happens to look over to the entrance area. She sees a guy coming into the hall, she **YELLS** and points to the guy, **"OH GOD, IT'S HIM!".**

Everyone looks over at the guy, the guy sees Carmen and tries to leave the hall, but Carlos **moves** like a cheetah and tackles him to the floor just as he reached the front door. Carlos punches the guy in the face and two of his fellow officers take the guy into custody. Carlos is nose to nose with the guy, "If I wasn't off duty, I'd book you myself. **Get him out of here!".**

The two officers escort the guy out of the hall and place him in one of the police cars outside. Carlos fixes his suit and goes back into the reception area. Raymond walks up to

Carlos, "That was my boy. I didn't want to come by myself and Crystal said it was okay to bring a friend".

Carlos raises his eyebrows, "A friend?". Raymond shakes his head, "I didn't know he…I didn't know. I'm sorry…*I'm really sorry*. Carlos pats Raymond on the back, "It's not your fault". Raymond shakes his head, "Man, this has been some evening". Carlos nods his head, "This has been some wedding. I hope the honeymoon is as exciting". They both smile at each other. Carlos looks over at his father. Carlos takes a deep breath and exhales.

Crystal walks over to Carlos, "Carlos, come with me". They walk over to Ramone, Crystal asks Ramone for the microphone and he hands it to her. "Excuse me, everyone. May I have your attention?. I have something to say. First, we want to apologize for the disturbance. You know as we get older, we are suppose to get wiser. However, that is not always the case. It is important that we have **understanding**. Understanding people, things and situations. This will help us to be better human beings. I hope some of us and you know *who* you are have learned from this experience. I know I have".

\*\*\*

Carlos takes the microphone from Crystal, "And so have I. Well…I don't know about you, but I came to have a good time and I think we should get back to what we came here for. Hit the music". Everyone claps and then heads back to the dance area.

The DJ puts on another song and Carlos escorts Crystal back to where they were dancing. Everyone starts dancing again. Carlos's father walks over to Raymond, "I'm extremely sorry for hitting you. Please forgive me?".

Carlos Sr. extends his hand to Raymond and Raymond raises his eyebrows, "I forgive you, if you forgive me". They both smile and shake hands. Carlos Sr. hugs Raymond and Raymond embraces him back. Crystal and Carlos happen to be looking at them and smile. Everyone in the hall are back to enjoying themselves, enjoying the festivities, enjoying life.

Well…this was quite an experience not just for Carlos, his father, mother, Crystal and Raymond, but for everyone. Everyone involved took away a **valued** lesson of life…**DON'T JUDGE A BOOK BY ITS COVER**. Only until you have read it thoroughly can you say whether you like it or not. Also, **LOVE** has its complexities and simplicities.

What makes each relationship unique is that each is……**ONE OF A KIND**.

# BIOGRAPHY

*Athena Dent* continues to do through her writing as she has done as a Teacher, Social Worker, Nursing Assistant and Mentoring: EMPOWERING others. Through the complexities and simplicities of the 'Human Spirit' came the success of her first novel, "Silk", which is being used to HEAL individuals, understand the relationship with one's self and with others. Her writing transcends age, gender, race and economic status.

In this novel, *One of a Kind Love*, the Human Spirit prevails again through the difficulties of life's challenges that people face from day to day. From this comes not just ENLIGHTENMENT, but CONFIRMATION.

CPSIA information can be obtained at www.ICGtesting.com
Printed in the USA
BVOW041750240213

314007BV00001B/138/P